THE GOINGS-ON IN GUILDHALL

Recollections of a Common Councilman of the City of London

THE GOINGS-ON IN GUILDHALL

*Recollections of a Common Councilman
of the City of London*

C Douglas Woodward

ATHENA PRESS
LONDON

The Goings-on in Guildhall
Recollections of a Common Councilman
of the City of London
Copyright © C Douglas Woodward 2008

ISBN 10-digit: 1 84748 226 0
ISBN 13-digit: 978 1 84748 226 6

First published 2008 by
ATHENA PRESS
Queen's House, 2 Holly Road
Twickenham TW1 4EG
United Kingdom

Printed for Athena Press

For Ann who shared the adventure

CONTENTS

1

THIS UNIQUE LOCAL AUTHORITY

This memoir is a highly personal account of civic affairs and the people involved in them within the Corporation of London, that somewhat mysterious and certainly unique local authority which runs the historic City of London, the 'Square Mile', and whose influence touches on so many aspects of London and indeed national life.

It is a record of my own greatly enjoyed participation, during the last thirty years of the twentieth century, as a member of the Court of Common Council, the City's governing body, which has been rightly described as one of the two finest clubs in the world (the other being the House of Commons).

It was a period that saw the disillusioned scrapping of Livingstone's Greater London Council and, at the end, his return as leader of a new London body but with the City itself and its Lord Mayor, so often over the centuries at odds with kings and Parliament, and from time to time under threat of abolition, still in being and seemingly flourishing. It has had long experience in the techniques of survival!

After all, City government had its foundations with the Romans, centuries earlier than Parliament, and developed under the Saxons. After the Norman

Conquest King William confirmed the rights and privileges that had been enjoyed by the citizens under Edward the Confessor. There emerged a commune, or corporation, with a Mayor at its head. By the mid-fifteenth century a 'modern' authority of Mayor, Aldermen and Commoners, or Councilmen, was firmly established – a pattern to be followed later by other towns and cities.

These historic roots and the adherence to them over the centuries are one of the reasons for the City's uniqueness as a local authority. Its separateness was strengthened by its medieval wall and, although the wall has almost entirely disappeared, anyone with a feeling for history can still sense its presence in keeping the City apart from its newer neighbours of Islington and Hackney and even from the other 'city' of Westminster. The dragons, which mark the entries into the City, are symbols of this continuing separateness.

There are more obvious differences between the City and the sprawling boroughs surrounding it: its size – small enough to walk from one end to the other in half an hour – and its tiny residential population. In the early 1970s, when my story begins, the City was also far wealthier than its neighbours and then, as now, could draw on private funds to maintain standards and undertake tasks beyond the abilities of other local authorities – a source of pride for City people but occasionally envy from those outside.

The City was and is the country's financial power-house, its banks and markets, brokers and dealers served by an army of commuters pouring in each day from the suburbs and farther afield. To protect its wealth-producing businesses (and to safeguard its citizens) the City has its own small and highly efficient police force.

Governing this quite special area, the Court of Common Council was also different in many ways from other councils. This little square mile had, in the 1970s, no fewer than 210 elected Aldermen and Councilmen so that its few residents and each of its business houses could expect to receive attentive service from their numerous elected representatives.

Elections to the Court were not every four years as everywhere else but took place annually in December, giving plenty of opportunity for change. The electoral process was different too, starting with the historic 'Ward Mote'. I will say more about this later.

The elected members had and have no political party affiliations – virtually the last stronghold in the country of true independents. They were and are unpaid, regarding their service to the City as an honour as well as a duty.

All these differences have led to misunderstanding in the world outside – and no little criticism, jealousy and challenge. When London government was last drastically refashioned, a Royal Commission stated in 1960: 'We propose that the City of London should remain as a separate entity. This is an anomaly but we recommend that this anomaly should continue, and we make this recommendation as a definite, not a provisional, recommendation.'

Alas, that was not to be the end of the story (as will be made clear later in my memoir), but at least in 2007, as I write these words, the anomaly that is the City is still there.

Most of the differences I have mentioned still remain but some recent changes are intended to make the City look more like ordinary London boroughs, these changes certainly prompted by a desire on the part of the Corporation to placate a Labour government and to give thanks for having been spared the abolition long promised by the Labour Party.

The most significant of these changes have been enlargement of the franchise giving votes to companies (sensible) and a substantial reduction in the number of Common Councilmen (wrong) with some wards reduced to having only two elected members compared with the five or six of earlier times. Overall, the number of Councilmen is down from 185 to 100 with the possibility of still further cuts.

2

CRIPPLEGATE RETURNS THE FIRST RESIDENTS TO COMMON COUNCIL

My wife, Ann, and I moved into the Barbican in April 1970, when fewer than a third of the flats had been completed and the Arts Centre was still a large hole in the ground. The resident population, still numbering only a few hundred, were invited that June to a meeting in the Golden Lane theatre (now offices) which had as its objective the establishment of a residents' association. The prime mover was Wilfrid Dewhirst, one of the very earliest of the Barbican Residents (he lived in Milton Court over the fire station there) and a member of the City's Metal Exchange.

Volunteers were called for to serve on the committee of this new 'Barbican Association'. I was one of the few people there actually known to another resident – the late Rosetta Desbrow – and she it was who unexpectedly volunteered me for the committee. Wilfrid Dewhirst became our first chairman. It was this involvement that was to lead both Dewhirst and myself into City government.

Later that year, Ann and I attended an election meeting in the City of London School for Girls which turned out to be our first introduction into the mysteries of how the City was run. On the platform were the twelve sitting members for our Ward of Cripplegate who were putting up for re-election in December. They appeared to us to be men of substance and *gravitas* – 'City Fathers' in the true sense of the word. They were clearly concerned as to the impact that these hundreds of new Barbican voters would have on their hitherto peaceful reign over Cripplegate whose electorate up to that time consisted of partners in the firms of accountants and solicitors doing business in the Ward, few of whom ever bothered to vote, plus a handful of resident caretakers and their wives in office blocks.

These twelve Councilmen lived in the suburbs (or further afield) and had become members of the Court of Common Council through having their businesses in Cripplegate and their membership of the Cripplegate Ward Club which at that time was the spawning ground and entrée for service on the Court. They were all 'City men', each being a member of at least one of the livery companies.

I must say a word now about politics in the City, about which I was still then woefully ignorant in spite of the fact that I had spent much of my working life in the City – in Fleet Street, Printing House Square (that ink-impregnated fortress of *The Times* in Blackfriars) and latterly in the insurance industry's headquarters at Aldermary House in Queen Street. Such ignorance was of course as common in those days as it is among City workers today!

The Ward of Cripplegate was one of twenty-six[1] wards, the boundaries of which were much the same in 1970 as in medieval times. Each of the Wards elected a number of Common Councilmen to represent its interests in the Court of Common Council and generally to engage in the government of the City. Each ward was administered by an Alderman who was elected just once 'for life'. Common Councilmen came up for election every year.

Elections were held, as they always had been, just before Christmas at the annual Ward Mote where residents and ratepayers could raise matters of concern and question the members putting up for election that year. The Alderman with his attendant beadle (Cripplegate had two) presided and the Ward Clerk (usually a local solicitor) conducted the business.

More often than not these elections were uncontested, the requisite number of contestants (twelve in Cripplegate) having offered themselves and being duly sworn in. Where there were additional candidates election was by show of hands, it then being open to an unsuccessful contestant (or any two ratepayers) to demand a poll with a secret ballot, which would take place the next day.

But now the long-standing arrangements in Cripplegate were to be challenged. Wilfrid Dewhirst had set his sights on becoming a member of the somewhat exclusive club that was the Court of Common Council and would use the new platform of the Barbican Association as his launch pad.

---

[1] The Ward of Bridge Without (taking in Southwark) only had an Alderman, no Common Councilmen, and would soon be amalgamated with the Ward of Bridge.

In June 1971, with a timely resignation from the Court of one of the old Cripplegate members, Dewhirst stood in a by-election with Ann and I acting as his 'agents'. He became the first Barbican resident to secure a Cripplegate seat on Common Council – a foretaste of things to come.

Ann and I not only attended at Guildhall to see him inducted as a Common Councilman, but were drawn by its pageantry – and by the quality of its debates – to go to the Court of Common Council where we were able to listen in from the public gallery at the back of Guildhall. Some of the discussions were of considerable interest to us – particularly those occasions when Alderman Edward Howard (soon to be Lord Mayor) and his supporters were campaigning to stop the Barbican Arts Centre from being built (they thought it a gross waste of ratepayers money) – far better to use the site for offices, they said. A by-product of this was that Ann and I, on behalf of the Barbican Association, organised a petition among residents asking the City Corporation to press on with the Arts Centre regardless.

I was now well and truly hooked by Guildhall and its goings-on and in October, with another by-election coming up, and with my own Barbican Association involvement as a platform, I threw my own hat into the ring as did two other residents – Leslie Fellner and Dennis Delderfield. Fellner, who had stood in June and lost to Wilfrid Dewhirst, was a man of principle and he did not win Barbican hearts when he wrote: 'It is up to these privileged tenants, in exchange for the facilities available to them, to do less complaining and make a positive contribution.' He did badly in the poll but Delderfield got six more votes than me and was the victor. He had sensibly remembered to canvass the caretakers in local offices and the livery halls, and their votes tipped the balance – a lesson I did not forget!

Presiding at the Ward Mote was that outstanding and most charismatic of Aldermen, Sir Peter Studd, who that year was Lord Mayor; he arrived that evening at the Ward Mote in all his mayoral splendour. His commiseration encouraged me to a second attempt at the December elections, when I and the other eleven sitting members were returned unopposed – the last time for many a year that Cripplegate would not have a contested election.

In January 1972, in the magnificent setting of the ancient Guildhall, accompanied by the Hallkeeper, I marched down the aisle past the rows of seated (and silent) Councilmen, bowing at various stages of our progress, ascended the dais to be welcomed by the new Lord Mayor – no other than Sir Edward Howard himself – as one of the Court's new intake. One was then robed by the Hallkeeper in a gown of mazarine blue borrowed for the occasion and, thus suitably dressed, marched back to one's place beside the other five Councilmen for Cripplegate Without.[2] On the walk back the assembly, as was the custom, clapped as an indication of their approval, at least one hoped that's what it was!

I was one of four inducted that day, the others being Brian Jenks, who with his wife Sue became our

---

[2] Although Cripplegate operated as a single Ward its historical division into Cripplegate Within (the wall) and Cripplegate Without remained.

friends; Iris Samuels, who joined her husband William and was to become the great champion for her Ward of Portsoken; and Christopher Mitchell who, with his brother, ran the renowned El Vino wine establishments in the City.

While members of the court were in their lounge suits, we new boys sweltered in our fur-trimmed gowns for what was to be one of the longest Court sittings ever, going on from 1 p.m. to 4.30 p.m. I wondered whether these lengthy sittings would often recur. If so, they could present difficulties for a working chap like me!

But on that day any anxiety was well and truly submerged in the glorious feeling of having arrived in a quite special place. Guildhall was to become almost a second home for the next twenty-five years and how fortunate I was that Ann would be such an enthusiastic participant in this brave new world.

3

THE COURT OF COMMON COUNCIL AT WORK

Since medieval times the City's Councilmen have always met in the ancient Guildhall or its immediate precincts. There were two earlier chambers dedicated to their meetings – George Dance's Council Chamber built in the late 1770s and demolished 1908, and Sir Horace Jones's twelve-sided Gothic-style Chamber of 1883–4 which was destroyed in the air raids of 1940. Since then the Court of Common Council has met in Guildhall itself, a truly grand setting which has the effect on new members of making them quickly realise how very small a cog they are in the machinery of City government.

Its architectural splendour and the historic pageantry of its proceedings set a standard for the quality of debate within these ancient walls. Laughter is by no means unheard here but overall there is an acceptance that this is an assembly where serious business is to be conducted in an atmosphere of grave formality.

In those days the Court met once a fortnight on alternate Thursdays. Guildhall was nearly always packed, the Councilmen seated row upon row in groups according to their wards. With 185 of us in 1972 our seats took up three quarters of the space in

Great Hall. Behind us was a barrier manned by the Keeper of the Guildhall and his assistants which hived us off from the public gallery at the back of the hall, which in those days was always well-filled.

A central gangway divided the groups of Councilmen and flanking this gangway were tables at which sat the Chairmen of the Corporation's twenty-two main committees. At the eastern end of Guildhall was the dais for the City's twenty-six (later twenty-five) Aldermen, the two Sheriffs and the High Officers – the Town Clerk who conducted the proceedings of the Court, the Chamberlain (nothing so ordinary as a treasurer or head of finance for the City), the Remembrancer (in charge of the City's ceremonial and liaison with Buckingham Palace and Parliament), the City Solicitor and Comptroller, the City Surveyor (responsible for the City's great property portfolio), the City Engineer, and the City Architect. The office of City Engineer has alas disappeared to be subsumed within a Department of Technical Services, and the City Architect has become the City Planning Officer – the march of progress! Harold King, City Engineer in 1972, was responsible for a new London Bridge. City Architects still designed buildings like the new City of London School on Queen Victoria Street.

Councilmen and Aldermen were expected to be in their places before 1 p.m. At precisely 'one of the clock' the Lord Mayor arrives having had a very early lunch at the Mansion House and been driven across to Guildhall in a Rolls Royce registration 'LM0'. He is attended by the Swordbearer who is in fur hat and carrying the ceremonial City sword, and the Common

Cryer and Serjeant-at-arms bearing the City mace.

The Lord Mayor in his finery begins his stately progress from the west door, past the rows of visitors and then through the assembled Councilmen who by this time are on their feet to applaud his entry. Swordbearer and Common Cryer remain at the foot of the dais ready to lay down the sword and mace while the Lord Mayor ascends the steps and moves to his throne-like seat at the centre. He doffs his hat to the Aldermen, Officers and Councilmen, and sits.

The Common Cryer, invariably a military man with powerful voice, calls: 'Oyez, Oyez, Oyez, will all members rise in their places', at which the Lord Mayor stands to deliver the Corporation prayer: *'Domine Dirige Nos'*. Business can now begin.

The scarlet robes of the Aldermen and mazarine blue of Councilmen are only worn on very special occasions at Council meetings, notably when a new Lord Mayor presides at his first Court early in November. Our finery is also worn when Guildhall is transformed into the venue for the great social occasions such as a new Lord Mayor's Banquet or when the City plays host to visiting kings and presidents – but more of that later.

Councilmen Had the Final Say

Although even in the 1970s the Corporation's business was conducted within its numerous committees, in those days most Committee recommendations came before the Court of Common Council for final approval, even some which seemed to us trivial. So it was that we members of the Court were empowered to

Common Council meeting 1883, in the twelve-sided Gothic-style chamber which survived until an air raid in 1940
Picture courtesy of Guildhall Library

Common Council one hundred years later in the
Great Hall of Guildhall.
Picture courtesy of London Metropolitan Archives

have our say and thus affect the Corporation's decision-making. Alas, it is all very different today with very few recommendations ever reaching the whole Court, and major decision-making taking place within a small inner group of chairmen and officers.

The difference could not be more marked than with the recommendations of the Planning Committee in respect of applications for building development within the City. In earlier years recommendations for approval of even quite modest new buildings always came to the Court where members having particular knowledge of the locality or having a particular view to express could comment and, not infrequently, get the recommendation 'referred back' to the Planning Committee for second thoughts – or even get it thrown out altogether.

After the City Heritage Society came into being in 1973 I found myself increasingly becoming spokesman for the cause of conservation – and was gratified to find that not just a few of my fellow members were of like mind. Thanks to our efforts a number of perfectly good Victorian and Edwardian buildings that had been threatened with demolition were saved and are still there today. I will later recount the most outstanding of all our planning battles – that relating to Number 1 Poultry.

The Court was called on to agree (or not) with each of the recommendations from committees. Disagreement was rare but if, perhaps after a couple of persuasive speeches from the floor, sufficient members held up their hands to disagree with the recommendation, the Town Clerk would count the number of hands held up and declare the result. If members then disagreed with his assessment, and provided that ten of them leapt to their feet, a division was called and bells rung with members filing off to left or right of the chamber to vote with the ayes or the noes, the Keeper of the Guildhall and his team counting the votes with tellers appointed to announce the result.

When I first joined, the Court divisions were infrequent but as the years went by and there were new members who took a more critical approach to Corporation affairs they occurred quite often. These days the division bells are very rarely heard in Guildhall – a pity in my view as indicating too great a willingness for members to go with the tide.

Our agendas were lengthy. I have mentioned my first Council meeting which lasted three-and-a-half hours, although two hours was more common. On a good day we might get away in not much more than an hour.

In addition to all the committee recommendations there were slots for questions to committee chairmen, and for any motions put down by the Town Clerk or members themselves.

Granting the 'Freedom of the City'

An early item at each Court of Common Council was approval of the list of people being recommended for the 'Freedom of the City' which we were asked to agree en bloc.

While Freedom of the City of London is an honour which the Corporation bestows upon great people – the Queen, the late Queen Mother, the Prince of Wales, prime ministers and military heroes – Nelson and Wellington – the Freedom is also sought by a host of ordinary people usually because of a particular connection with or attachment to the City. This privilege grew from the requirement in earlier times that for anyone who wanted to exercise a trade or craft within the City, the Freedom was an essential prerequisite. To this day, the Freedom is a necessary qualification for the holding of civic office – Alderman, Sheriff or Common Councilman – and remains a requirement for admission to any one of the City's hundred-plus livery companies.

Generally our agreement to the names being put forward was never in doubt, but I do recall occasions when condemnatory remarks were made (usually in respect of a politician whose views were not to everyone's taste). But the great majority of us were usually too good-natured to delete even those names from the roll of honour. I should add that the cost of Freedom by redemption or purchase has gone up from the few pounds of my day to £30 today. The proceeds go towards the cost of running the City of London Freemen's School in Ashstead Park, Surrey. Residents in the City may claim the Freedom without charge.

4

THE FINEST CLUB IN THE WORLD – AND A RIPOSTE TO A LABOUR PARTY ATTACK

1972, and my first year as a member of the Court of Common Council. The Deputy for my ward of Cripplegate Without was the seventy-nine-year-old Ernest Parker who had himself been elected to the Court in 1952 and had served as Ward Deputy for ten years. Each of the City's twenty-five wards had a Deputy (i.e. Deputy to the Alderman of the Ward) whose job it was to arrange the business of the ward and – in those days, anyway – to keep his fellow members on the straight and narrow. In general the Deputy was the longest serving member of the ward. In Cripplegate we had two Deputies, one for Without and one for Within.

Ernest, a true City character, liveryman of no fewer than three Companies – the Bakers, Gold and Silver Wyre Drawers and the Horners – past Master of Cripplegate Ward Club, and past President of the United Wards Club, had a word of advice: 'Don't open your mouth in Common Council for at least a year.' He appointed me to two Corporation Committees: the Planning Committee which I was delighted to get (it wasn't a favourite with the other members with its fortnightly meetings and lengthy agendas), and Billingsgate and Leadenhall Markets Committee with its more relaxed monthly get-togethers.

The Billingsgate Committee was fun, and I remember in particular our early morning tours of inspection of the Old Billingsgate Market in Lower Thames Street led by the Clerk and Superintendent, Charles Wiard (one-time Olympic rowing star), where we picked our way though the fish stalls to admire some of the exotic catch from Far Eastern waters alongside eels and octopi. These splendid visits concluded with 'breakfast' in the Superintendent's office where the chief delicacy was a Dover sole on the bone spilling over the edges of the large plate.

Billingsgate Market in its heyday in Lower Thames Street
Picture courtesy of London Metropolitan Archives

The Chairman of the Billingsgate Committee was unusual in that he was an Alderman – a very rare occurrence in those days. Christopher Rawson was stout, somewhat choleric, and an extremely good chairman, devoted to the well-being of the fish market. He had already served as 'lay' Sheriff (as opposed to Aldermanic Sheriff) some years earlier and by rights should by 1972 have been well along the road to becoming lord mayor. Alas, for reasons never made public, Rawson was not favoured by the Court of Aldermen and, as had happened in the past and would happen again to future Aldermen, his progression was halted with others taking on the office of Aldermanic Sheriff ahead of him but he soldiered on as the Alderman for Lime Street Ward.

Another of the Aldermen would a year or two later find his progress towards the mayoralty coming to an end even though he had jumped the first big hurdle of becoming Aldermanic Sheriff. I remember a conversation with him and some others at a reception in Fishmongers' Hall on London Bridge when he said of himself that whilst a most tolerant man he could well do without Jews and blacks. The drinks had been flowing pretty freely!

The Planning Committee was something else. As I have said, we met once every two weeks under the benevolent, if somewhat strict, chairmanship of solicitor Frank Steiner, later to be a highly-regarded Chief Commoner. Even in those far-off days I had conservationist leanings and was far from enamoured at the way in which the City's Victorian buildings were increasingly coming under attack. My somewhat puny interventions met with surprised incredulity on the part of the Chairman and were usually fairly quickly squashed in a committee where development was the order of the day and conservation regarded as a bit odd.

But I had some friends there including Alderman Sir Ian Bowater, one of the City's grandees, lord mayor not long since, who decided I was an ally in his constant campaign to rid the City of its last remaining bomb sites, one or two of which were still there in 1972.

In spite of my Deputy's instruction to stay silent at meetings of Common Council I found it difficult not to join in the debates at Guildhall. Indeed both Dennis Delderfield and I were fairly soon on our feet when we felt we had something useful to contribute. So far as I can remember, his first offering was during discussion of the City of London Festival, his suggestion being that alongside the Bach, Vivaldi and Handel, why not have some lighter moments such as brass bands in Paternoster Square.

It was something of a challenge to speak for the first time in crowded Guildhall when, having got to your feet you waited for the Town Clerk to call your name (hoping that he might conceivably recognise such a new face) and then making your way to the nearest microphone. One had taken note of the correct procedure and began with the words: 'My Lord Mayor...' and knowing full well that one was addressing an audience who, while extremely polite, did not bear fools gladly. After the first few goes one got into the swing of it and even began rather to enjoy speaking in Guildhall. Some of the older members may have got up to speak too often and one in particular clearly felt himself to be a latter-day Churchill addressing the House of Commons. To make up for their loquacity, though, at least half the 185 members had never spoken in Common Council and never would.

Labour Party Has a Go at the City

In March 1972 Tony Banks (later an MP), with support from other left-wingers, led the latest full-scale attack on the City Corporation calling for its abolition as a unit of local government. The battle-ground was the letters page of *The Times*. Horace Cutler, then Conservative leader of the Greater London Council (and I) replied.

Cutler said in his letter that Tony Banks' party was 'committed to the abolition of the City Corporation and the House of Lords and there was growing pressure for the abolition of the monarchy. The objective is a grey, sombre and ostensibly "classless" society and the strategy is to knock over these institutions one by one.'

In my letter from the Members' Room at Guildhall, I wrote:

Mr Banks has again made clear the Labour Party's intent to abolish the City of London Corporation as a separate unit of local government. He gives the impression that the City Corporation is a collection of rotten boroughs. The truth of the matter is that the City Corporation is among the most efficient of local authorities. Our own housekeeping is such that our rates demand for City services is among the lowest in the country.

The accusation that we are not democratic is absurd if one takes into account the fact that we elect our councillors every twelve months. Admittedly we have rather a lot of councillors for our small area but that surely is not a bad matter especially since we are the only council in the country whose members do not receive any attendance allowance.

Compare City local government with what is going on in places like Lambeth and Camden where Mr Banks' friends preside and you can see why they look with envious and destructive eyes at the way we conduct our affairs.

Such responses as these may have helped to quell (for the time being at least) further attacks on the City – but they would certainly recur.

Another Election

At the end of 1972 a contested Cripplegate election was pending, as was to be the case year after year in our ward. Oddly enough, one became quite accustomed to these annual elections just before Christmas, in spite of the task of having to produce an election address and delivering it to the nearly 3,000 addresses in the Barbican and to the office partnerships on the electoral roll – all at a time of year when potential voters had other things on their minds!

It was all much easier and more agreeable because of the friendship we felt towards the other Cripplegate members – so much so that in my early years on the Court the sitting members seeking to be re-elected produced a common election address which, in 1972, featured all twelve of us complete with passport-type photographs, dates of birth and marital status. With my newspaper and PR background I soon found myself charged with producing these election addresses year after year.

The Ward Mote and subsequent poll were at the Chartered Insurance Institute in Aldermanbury where Ann and I, with other members, took turns at manning a table where we marked off the names of voters, something which could not happen in today's more politically correct climate but seemed to be enjoyed by those bothering to vote as making more of an occasion of it.

On 21 December, the *City of London Recorder* (we had our own splendid local newspaper in those days) under the heading 'Cripplegate Shock' announced that Ernest Parker and Leslie Walshaw Smith, two of the Cripplegate stalwarts, had lost their seats, Ernest having been a Councilman for twenty years and Leslie for fourteen – most distressing, if not totally unexpected, for them both. The two new members were both Barbican residents, Leslie Fellner (at the third attempt) and Brigadier John Packard. Voting that year was something of a record at 23% of the electorate. As was to be the case for a good many years I found myself, much to my surprise, topping the poll.

'The Finest Club in the World'

I had greatly enjoyed my first year on Common Council. There was the friendship with Cripplegate colleagues and with a growing number of other members of the Court whom one met in Committee or full Council. And of course one enjoyed the numerous social occasions that have always been a feature of the City: the dinners provided by the Chairmen of Committees (indeed I had the Planning Committee Dinner even before attending my first meeting of the Committee); the Spring and Autumn State Banquets at Guildhall given for visiting kings and presidents; the dinners at the Mansion House for the bishops, judges and masters of livery companies; and of course the great Banquet at Guildhall given in November by the new Lord Mayor and Sheriffs and attended by the Prime Minister, Archbishop of Canterbury, and the Lord Chancellor, together with over 700 other guests.

Members of the Court, all 185 of us, had invitations (with our wives) to all these splendid occasions, feeling ourselves greatly privileged – and not just a little important!

Together with the camaraderie, enjoying such great occasions (in the knowledge that not a single one of these was a charge on the rates) were reasons enough why we Councilmen knew ourselves to be members of the finest club in the world! Little wonder that members tended to stay on into their eighties and beyond.

5

CRIPPLEGATE NOTABILITIES, THE BIRTH OF CITY HERITAGE AND A FIRST TRY FOR A CITY LOTTERY

The Cripplegate members arriving for the early Court of Common Council business in January 1973 were the best of friends. Our Alderman remained Sir Peter Studd. Cripplegate Within had as its deputy, John Henderson, a textile merchant (whose father before him had held the same office) already on the Court for more than ten years. In my own part of the Ward, Cripplegate Without, Wallis Hunt (stockbroker and father of racing driver James), also with ten years' service, was Deputy. Both John and Wallis were later to achieve the exalted rank of Chief Commoner. The others were much-liked Stanley Chubb (accountant), Budge Brooks (best known of City wine merchants with cellarage in the old Wood Street Comptor, one-time prison for debtors), Derek Balls, managing director of famous Balls Bros wine bars, Charles Coward, most civilised of property men (with Wimbledon Centre Court tickets for his friends), and Harold Titchener, highly respected printer and block-maker. These were the seven remaining 'business' members of the ward. By now there were five

Barbican residents: Wilfrid Dewhirst, Dennis Delderfield, Leslie Fellner, John Packard and myself.

In my view, Cripplegate, with more than 600 business voters on the electoral roll, was well served by having this mixture to represent it at Guildhall but not everyone in the Barbican was of that way of thinking and pressure was clearly growing to turn the Cripplegate wards into largely, if not wholly, Barbican fiefdoms. This process was of course facilitated by the fact that Barbican residents were more easily persuaded to go to the polls than were the partners in the firms of stockbrokers, accountants and lawyers occupying the office blocks within the ward who saw little benefit to themselves in bothering to turn out to vote.

We did try, all of us, to encourage greater business participation, particularly in the December elections. It meant finding someone – if possible the senior partner in the firm – who would accept a parcel of election addresses and distribute them to their fellow partners. Even then, unless there were exceptional circumstances (such as one of the partners actually standing for election), the response was invariably poor.

Even in the Barbican, as the years went by, with elections every December, the first flush of enthusiasm soon died away. I have mentioned the 23% turnout in the 1972 election. During the remainder of the 1970s we managed to maintain good turnouts of between 15% and 20% but once into the 1980s the voting figures were to fall away to around 10%. My highest personal vote was 333 in 1975 with John Packard close behind on 324. That year 398 people voted out of a total electorate of 2,467 – that is 16%.

In Cripplegate we tended in December to look with some envy at our colleagues in other wards who were only infrequently obliged to compete in an election. Our suggestion that elections should be on a four-year cycle like other boroughs fell, not surprisingly, on deaf ears – the other members were happy with things as they were! In 2005 the Corporation did, in fact, go over to four-yearly elections to prove to Downing Street that it really was no different to other authorities, a great pity in my view, a change not for the better of anyone.

For some reason I cannot now recall, the system of having a joint election address was dropped just once, in December 1973. My personal election address this year noted I had by then lived in the Barbican for nearly four years and had served on the Committee of the Barbican Association since its inception. With Ann's help we had established a Barbican Association clubroom near our flat in Gilbert House where bridge, French conversation and performances by Guildhall School students took place, and a full range of drinks were served in the evenings. I became adept at man-handling the beer casks. Two waitresses from my office luncheon mess helped out and members of the committee were there to tot up the evening's takings. Also, for the Barbican Association, Ann and I organised annual winter gatherings which took place in local pubs, attendance never being below a couple of hundred. All this meant one got to know a large number of Barbican residents – and they got to know me, which was clearly a factor in the number of votes I received in the annual elections!

The Birth of City Heritage

In the Planning Committee we were in the process of establishing a Conservation Area Advisory Committee to protect the City's eight 'conservation areas' from inappropriate development. It seemed to me that residents should have a place on that committee along-side the representatives of ward clubs and more commercially-minded interests. In something of a rush, Tony Henfrey (another Barbican resident) and I formed the Barbican Association Conservation Group so that we could nominate a representative to attend the first meeting of the new Conservation Area Advisory Committee in April. Barbican residents, many of whom were not enamoured with City building development in the 1970s, responded with enthusiasm and membership of our conservation group grew quickly to more than 300. The Barbican Association Conservation Group was to become the City Heritage Society, the City's widely respected amenity and conservation body, now in its thirty-fourth year.

My 1973 election address was therefore able, with some justification, to say that I was 'actively promoting preservation and improvement of the few old parts of the City still left', and was seeking more residential accommodation in the City (something of a pioneering thought at that time).

A City Lottery Mooted and London Bridge Sold to the Americans

In 1973 there was much talk of lotteries on a small scale and in January I had put down a motion in the

Court of Common Council urging the City to consider running a lottery to help ease the rates burden. The motion was seconded by an old friend, Ivan Luckin, who a couple of years earlier had kindly sponsored me for the Freedom of the City – a requirement if one wanted to stand for Common Council, although at that time I had no such aspirations.

Ivan, a lovely man, member of the Needlemakers' livery company and a representative of Candlewick Ward, was to have a particular claim to fame for it was he who had the brilliant idea, when Rennie's London Bridge of 1831 was to be replaced, of offering it for sale in the United States. In two trips to New York he clinched a deal for the City with Robert P. McCullogh, an American property magnate. The bridge would be demolished stone by stone and shipped to Lake Havasu, Arizona, there to be rebuilt to span the Colorado River specially diverted for this purpose. The whole incredible enterprise resulted in a bit of Arizona desert being turned into a new city and successful tourist attraction with London Bridge as its central feature. The story that the American buyer – a very astute businessman – thought he was buying Tower Bridge was quite untrue!

Back to that lottery motion. There was a lengthy debate in Common Council with some older members saying that lotteries were not in keeping with the traditions and integrity of the Court. In a division my motion was narrowly defeated – fifty-seven votes to fifty. But that was not to be the end of the story.

6

A MOVEMENT FOR REFORM – AND SOME NOTABILITIES AMONG ALDERMEN AND COMMONERS

In 2007, with the City Corporation lamenting the state of its finances, it is interesting to recall that back in 1974 the then Chairman of the Coal, Corn and Rates Finance Committee (what a shame that it is now merely called the Finance Committee!), James Keith, was making exactly the same complaint – projects having to be postponed, highway improvements in jeopardy, economy the order of the day. As today, the vast sums collected by the Corporation in business rates went straight to the Exchequer.

What else was happening in the City in 1974? We had an early IRA bomb at the Tower of London with the victims carried to Barts – then, of course, a real hospital, the most famous in the land. In the Barbican the blocks of flats were being completed and filling up. The Arts Centre however remained a large hole in the ground.

The Library Committee announced that the Cripplegate Library, then in Golden Lane, would have to close and there would be no replacement until new premises became available in the Arts Centre – still years away. The Cripplegate Councilmen argued in the committee and then in Common Council that Barbican and other users could not be thus deprived of reading matter and won agreement for a temporary library to be created on the highwalk opposite Barbican. Joy all round.

The hoped-for new fish market in Docklands was badly delayed because the government and GLC had been more dilatory than usual in granting a development permit for the offices we needed over the market. By the time the permit arrived, the current economic crisis had put a stop to local authority borrowing. Old Billingsgate would continue for a good many years.

In planning we were seeing some happy signs for conservation with agreement on refurbishment of narrow Bow Lane and closing it to traffic; the Bank conservation area greatly extended; and plans for Carter Lane buildings to be restored rather than totally redeveloped. To help small businesses the Planning Committee were persuaded that in some of the new office developments floor space should be divided into small, less expensive units, suitable for solicitors, insurance brokers, surveyors and accountants.

A Richness of Aldermen

Looking around Guildhall on Common Council days I was greatly impressed by the presence of so many seemingly superior beings – some of the Commoners around me and more particularly the Aldermen seated upon the dais. The title of 'Alderman' has long since disappeared from every other local authority in the country but in the City it remains as an extremely important part of City government since it is from among the Aldermen that the Lord Mayor is elected each year. So it is that in the City there are two quite separate and distinct 'streams' – the Common Councilmen elected annually (until the year 2005) and the Aldermen, one for each of the City's twenty-five wards, who until recently were elected for life (or at least until they reached the age of seventy when they were obliged to retire being also magistrates). An Alderman, when seeking election was, in effect, declaring his intention (or at least his hope) one day of becoming Lord Mayor of London. It was – if all went well – a lengthy progression lasting some twelve years in which around his ninth or tenth year he would be elected as the Aldermanic Sheriff (a second 'lay' Sheriff would be elected alongside him) and three years later would be elected Lord Mayor.

Our Aldermen included such people as Denis Truscott, Ralph Perring, Robert Bellinger – a roll call of wealthy and influential City men, all having served as Lord Mayor of London, each having received right at the start of their mayoralty a baronetcy or having been appointed a Knight Grand Cross of the Most Excellent Order of the British Empire (GBE). There too was Sir Bernard Waley-Cohen, a tank of a man, Alderman for the traditionally Jewish ward of Portsoken. He rode to hounds with a Devon hunt, introduced a new Midsummer banquet at Mansion House and made some good speeches, but in his later years tended to be a bit of a battering ram if you were standing in his way. Sir Hugh Wontner was the colourful owner of the Savoy Hotel and could be rather grand.

Moves for Reform

'The 1974 Group' set up that year was the brainchild of half-a-dozen members who felt that the Corporation stood in need of some urgent reforms. One of the moving spirits who became its chairman was Fred Cleary, most delightful and civilised of property developers, who became a great friend with whom we dined at his flat in Grosvenor Square or sipped champagne on a Sunday morning at his house in St Margaret's Bay.

Others were Alderman Alan Traill (to be Lord Mayor in 1984) and Peter Rigby, who came to the City after a successful political career in the borough of Hornsey and was never without a Guildhall chairmanship. One or two newcomers – Denis Delderfield, Leslie Fellner and I – were roped in as potential movers and shakers.

'The 1974 Group' proposed a dozen or so reforms intended to make the City work more efficiently and to help silence the criticism that came from outside as to the miniscule number of voters on the roll in many of our wards. Two of these proposed reforms were to enlarge the franchise by giving votes to limited companies according to the amount of business rates they paid, and to rearrange the boundaries between wards so as to spread the electorate out more evenly. These ideas we promoted in Common Council but successive chairmen of our Policy and Parliamentary Committee strongly advised us to 'let sleeping dogs lie' and not draw the attention of the House of Commons to controversial aspects of City government and which would entail legislation at Westminster for any change to be made. Appeals made later to Conservative Home Secretaries drew the same kind of response – 'keep your heads below the parapet', we were advised.

It is perhaps ironic that it was not until the new millennium, with a Labour government in office, that these selfsame reforms were finally adopted by the House of Commons in the teeth of opposition from a few rabid left-wingers who still hankered after the City's abolition, not its reform! It thus took just on thirty years to achieve the key reforms first advanced in 1974.

'The 1974 Group' was somewhat critical of the Court of Aldermen, rather more a power in the land in those days, and we even had ideas for improvement of the mayoralty. The main complaint was the way in which the Court of Aldermen, without giving any reason, would occasionally turn down the candidature of someone who aspired to join them – or, in the case of an existing Alderman, block his progress to becoming Lord Mayor. I have already mentioned one or two such cases.

So it was arranged that a deputation of some six of us, led by Fred Cleary, should put our concerns to the Lord Mayor over tea at the Mansion House. Sir Hugh Wontner it was who received us and though urbanely charming as always, he made it abundantly clear to us that criticism of the Aldermen was unwelcome and that they had a duty to keep out anyone they considered unsuitable. He reminded us that the Lord Mayor, during his year in office, 'was regarded as minor royalty with all the privileges and responsibilities which that entailed'. Our eyebrows may have risen but I must say I found his total assurance impressive and, indeed, reassuring. With someone like Hugh Wontner up there no one would have the nerve to upstage the City of London.

It was he who, in 1976, was to found the Temple Bar Trust which many years later would be instrumental in securing the return of Temple Bar to the City.

Leslie Fellner followed Fred Cleary in leading the 1974 Group although he modestly described himself as convener rather than chairman, and I followed Leslie. With quite a few of our ideas having at least become talking points at Guildhall I felt able to recommend that the group be disbanded a year or two later.

Notable Commoners

I have mentioned some of the Aldermen of the day. What of the so-called Commoners? We had Colin Cole, Garter King of Arms representing Castle Baynard Ward; Bunny Morgan, who was undoubtedly the best known man of the civic City and, indeed, synonymous with it; Gordon Wixley who would become a distinguished Chairman of the Policy Committee; Norman Harding from Asprey's the jewellers, enormously popular and a future Chief Commoner; George Vine, whose long and dedicated chairmanship of the troubled Barbican Committee eventually led to a breakdown in his health; Norman Hall, a solicitor in Cloth Fair much liked and another future Chief Commoner, and many others of note.

'Deputation' of Common Councilmen, in gowns and carrying our wands of office, processing into a Mansion House luncheon

There were only three lady members out of 185 in my early days: Iris Samuels, who came on to the Court on the same day as I had done, joining her husband William in their fiefdom of Portsoken; Mary Donaldson, the first of the few, soon to get a committee chairmanship, later becoming Alderman and Sheriff and Lord Mayor in 1983; and Edwina Coven, wartime army major and another Chief Commoner in the making, but whose aspirations towards becoming an Alderman were blocked by the

Court of Aldermen, for which she would never forgive them.

In the December elections of 1974, John Henderson, one of our Cripplegate Deputies, lost his seat in Common Council to Barbican resident Donald Silk, someone whose name was later to become quite famous within the City and far beyond. John had dinner with Ann and me in our flat on election night and I think he was not unaware of the turning tide. But when the results were announced he was totally devastated, feeling that his long years of service to Cripplegate and the City had been ungratefully dismissed. For months afterwards he would attend the fortnightly meetings of Common Council as a member of the public 'to keep his hand in'. The following year we were all pleased to see him welcomed as a member for the Ward of Langbourn where he was to stay as a Deputy for many years.

Thus in Cripplegate we now had six Barbican Residents and six remaining from the business sector. Much as some of us regretted it, for those six the warning signals were now all too apparent.

7

LET'S SCRAP THE PROFLIGATE GREATER LONDON COUNCIL

Londoners in 1975 were just starting to realise what a millstone the Greater London Council had become in the ten years since its creation in 1965, a time when 'bigness' in London government was all the rage and we saw such excellent boroughs as Holborn, St Pancras, Hampstead and Finsbury amalgamated into amorphous monsters like Camden and Islington.

Sitting on top of these vast new conurbations was the Greater London Council covering both the inner London boroughs and the sprawling new outer ones such as Barnet, Bromley, and Bexley. A new Inner London Education Authority (ILEA) was also created at this time.

Sad to say it was the Conservative government which gave birth to these overblown authorities, doubtless hoping that so far as the GLC was concerned the conservative leanings of the Barnets, Bexleys and Bromleys would counter and outvote the left-leaning inclinations of the inner boroughs – a hope that would in any event be dashed all too soon.

Within a few years of its creation this 'slim and inexpensive' GLC as it was originally conceived, particularly after a change from Conservative to Labour control, had expanded to become a London-wide threat.

We were especially hard-hit in the City with soaring rates bills for both businesses and residents. Guildhall's own rates demands remained modest, the villains of the piece being the GLC and its equally voracious partner, the ILEA.

So it was that my particular hobby horse in 1975 was to begin a campaign about our rates bills. Looking back now over the 1970s and 1980s I am really quite proud of my own contribution in helping to bring down the GLC. I have to say that my experience of that earlier attempt at big London government made me highly sceptical as to the benefits to be derived from a Labour government's second model of the same presided over (as was the GLC) by Mr Livingstone!

My publicly voiced concerns in the newspapers led the Conservative Bow Group to invite a contribution from me to their influential *CrossBow* magazine:

The particular reasons why the GLC must go are that it is demonstrably inefficient – presiding as it does over the collapse of services for which it has responsibility – planning, transport and housing; that it has got completely out of control of the Londoners who elect it, having outrageously exceeded the guidelines set for it; and that it is the very epitome of the profligate public authority which is at the root of our economic ills.

Today the slim, inexpensive body has a budget which has soared from £193 million to an unbelievable £1,500 million. The GLC staff, too big when it started, is now around the 35,000 level (excluding London Transport and the ILEA). The salary bill has jumped from £87 million a year ago to £123 million currently. The GLC has not only filled the old London County Council at County Hall and the Middlesex County Council headquarters, but still short of space for its army of officials has built itself another vast extension.

All this, I wrote, was the reason why London's rates had increased twice as much as elsewhere in Britain. While the boroughs tried to economise the GLC's precept kept on growing – 85% up in 1974 and another 80% up in 1975. The only solution as I saw it was to scrap the GLC.

What should be the alternative? I suggested in *CrossBow* that the big London boroughs were large enough to run their own affairs and that co-ordination could be effected through the existing London Boroughs Association.

Somewhat more controversially, I told *CrossBow* readers that for most of the nineteenth century the government was forever pleading with the City Corporation to take over government of the whole of London – pleas to which the City, all too content to stay with its historic responsibilities for the Square Mile, turned a deaf ear.

Bearing in mind the admirable way the City conducts its affairs, its strictly non-political make-up and the esteem with which it appears to be regarded by its borough neighbours, it might well be appropriate for the City, a century later, at least to provide the venue and servicing facilities for co-ordination of the boroughs' activities.

Illtyd Harrington was quite liked as Labour Chairman of the GLC in 1975 but even he was not an over-welcome guest in Guildhall or Mansion House on the rare occasions it was felt necessary for the Corporation to invite the GLC to attend a Council meeting or a dinner. Of course, later with Ken Livingstone as his successor, the groundswell of opposition to the GLC would grow far stronger.

Meanwhile in Guildhall

Meanwhile in Guildhall our Policy and Parliamentary Committee was responding to yet another Labour Party call for abolition of the City Corporation.

More agreeably Lord Mayor Lindsey Ring had opened a new west wing at Guildhall, a stylish building running along Aldermanbury and fronting on to Guildhall Yard. Within it our committees were provided with handsome committee rooms and much-improved accommodation for the Town Clerk and other staff.

Particularly welcomed by the members of Common Council was a new Guildhall Club, (complete with bar), where Councilmen were given lunch either at the conclusion of a morning committee or before attending an afternoon one. Managing this splendid new enterprise with great flair was Doreen Briggs, who happily stayed with us until the end of 2006.

On the planning front, Whitbread's were proposing to turn their now unwanted brewery in Chiswell

Street into a conference and entertainment centre. They promised to provide stables for their splendid team of dray horses (recruited each November to haul the coach for the Lord Mayor's Show) over the road in Whitecross Street but alas this was never to happen, although Barbican did get its first supermarket there as consolation.

In Cripplegate we had started the year with a newly-conceived Ward Service, brainchild of Denis Delderfield, with a procession of Alderman, Common Councilmen, Masters of the livery companies having halls in our ward, and other dignitaries received at the parish church of St Giles by the rector, Edward Rogers, ex-Navy Chaplain.

We had a Cripplegate Festival in the summer with hundreds of residents and office workers sampling the attractions of stalls on St Giles' Terrace and cheering the opening ceremony of 'Beating the Bounds' of Cripplegate but lacking, alas, any choirboys to toss in the air.

Wallis Hunt was elected Chief Commoner, the first Cripplegate man to lead Common Council for twenty years, following his chairmanship of the Music Committee, his dinners in the Guildhall crypt with musical entertainment by students from the Guildhall School becoming a highlight of the City's social scene.

That year we lost Stanley Chubb and Charles Coward, another two of our 'business' representatives from Common Council, and were soon to get our first two lady members – Ninette Thompson who was in and out again quite quickly, and Rosemary Humphrays, who stayed for a good many years and was to hold more than one chairmanship.

8

LOTTERY IS ANOTHER CITY 'FIRST' AND WE KEEP UP THE PRESSURE ON RATES

While 1976 in the City was overshadowed by continuing economic gloom, there were all manner of excitements in Guildhall, not least for the Cripplegate members.

We said farewell to Sir Peter Studd, our distinguished Alderman for the past sixteen years on reaching the Aldermanic retirement age of seventy. We welcomed our newly elected Alderman Allan Davis who, with his wife Pam, were popular Barbican neighbours, thus beginning a new chapter of Aldermanic distinction.

In May, two days after the Home Secretary had given the all-clear for local authority lotteries, my second attempt for a City lottery, narrowly defeated the first time, was approved by Common Council and we thus became the very first local authority in the country to launch such a scheme. Asked in an LBC radio interview how Guildhall had been so quick off the mark, I said that the City of London was always ahead of the field! I meant it, too.

We looked to make a modest £100,000 a year from

ticket sales, the proceeds going to help fund good causes including the City of London Archaeological Trust (of which years later I was to become chairman) and that splendid City institution the Mermaid Theatre at Puddle Dock beside Blackfriars Bridge. The Mermaid's moving spirit was the actor and producer Bernard Miles, who was always on the lookout for a bit more money to keep his somewhat precarious enterprise afloat. In those days two of you could enjoy an excellent dinner in the Mermaid restaurant, with Bernard and his handsome wife Josephine as neighbours, followed by one of his memorable shows, all for ten pounds.

At St Giles Church the City Heritage Society staged an exhibition on building conservation in the City, opened in some style with my arrival on a vintage fire engine with bells ringing. City Heritage, still in its early days, was concentrating on maintaining the City's ancient passages, alleyways and lanes. Our exhibition highlighted the importance of refurbishing the buildings along Bow Lane and Lovat Lane and our efforts certainly helped to keep the quality of both, although our proposals to turn Lovat Lane off Eastcheap into a place of apartments and cafes never came off. We were ahead of our time on that one.

Residents Rise Up Against their Rates Bills

In April, with new rates demands going through the ceiling, it was time to have another go at the GLC. Residents were up in arms and the Barbican Association, chaired by Stella Currie, organised a

protest meeting in the City of London Girls' School –
a favoured venue for such gatherings – which I was
asked to chair.

We had on the platform Gerald Stitcher, Chairman
of the Corporation's Coal, Corn and Rates Finance
Committee, who had a few days before told the Court
of Common Council that nearly 90% of the rates
collected in the City went to the GLC and ILEA.

To the 400 residents packed that night into the
school he said: 'You are being sacrificed more than any
other ratepayers in London.' Another complaint was
levelled by him at the Rates Equalisation Scheme by
which the 'rich' boroughs in inner London were
forced to plough millions a year into a fund to help the
'poor' outer boroughs like Richmond and Sutton – a
glaring nonsense if ever there was one!

In my speech I declared that domestic rates had
more than doubled and that soaring business rates
were forcing smaller firms to close down and bigger
ones to move – not at all good for the City's health.
The vast bulk of these increases were to meet Greater
London needs. In 1970, our ratepayers had contributed
£22 million, that figure itself more than enough, but by
1976 the demand had risen to £140 million – the
villains being the Greater London Council and the
Inner London Education Authority which between
them took nearly all the rates collected in the City.

The City also suffered because of its tiny residential
population. The government's rate support grant,
intended to ease the burden for domestic ratepayers,
was based on residential population; that the City also
looked after 300,000 commuters was ignored.

Government grant was therefore miniscule.

So that night we agreed to launch an immediate protest to the government accompanied by a petition (with 500 signatures) which our MP, Christopher Tugendhat, would deliver to Peter Shore, then Secretary of State for the Environment. This is what the petition said:

> We the undersigned, residents in the City of London, wish to draw to your attention the onerous rates which we suffer and which arise from a disastrous combination of circumstances: namely, extremely high rateable values resulting in extremely high rates precepts for Greater London needs, and a very small resident population resulting in minimal rate support grant. The government's efforts to cushion ratepayers are thus nullified in our case and we therefore petition you to alleviate the burden on domestic ratepayers in the City of London by some adjustment in the government subvention, bearing in mind that last year our rates bill rose by 65% and that this year by are due to rise by a further 17%.

Closing the meeting I forecast that, 'Tonight will see the beginning of a continuous protest against excessive spending by the GLC and ILEA, the unfairness of the Rates Equalisation Scheme and the particular unfairness of the present rating system as it affects residents in the City.'

That protest would continue for a good few years. Our actions that April, combined with representations from Guildhall, were shortly to bear their first fruit with an acceptance by government that City residents were indeed unfairly treated and the drawing up of a formula which would take our particular circumstances into account in fixing the rates.

And Another Protest over Rent Rises

In the Barbican substantial rent increases had sparked off a disquietingly large number of tenants packing up and leaving. These were the days before Margaret Thatcher introduced the 'right to buy' for tenants of local authority housing and quite a few of the original occupants of Barbican flats saw the financial sense of owning their own housing – hence the exodus.

So it was that in October 1976 we had another protest meeting in the Girl's School where a resolution calling on the Lord Mayor and Corporation to consider the exodus from the Barbican and to draw up plans to 'stop the rot' was carried by more than 400 residents who packed themselves into the hall that evening – many standing in the aisles and at the back of the hall.

The following week, Wallis Hunt, as Deputy for the Ward, presented the resolution to the Court of Common Council calling on the Corporation's Policy and Parliamentary Committee urgently to examine the problem. This was the first occasion when the concerns of Barbican residents were put before Common Council. It would certainly not be the last.

Around the City

The Court of Common Council this year changed from fortnightly to three-weekly meetings with still more tightly packed agendas.

The Barbican Development Committee had drafted in some 500 construction workers to try to get things moving more quickly on the much delayed Arts and Conference Centre with completion now promised for 1979. Frobisher Crescent, which was to have provided the Barbican's only shops, was commandeered for extra Arts Centre office accommodation. I sought to persuade the committee that the restaurant facilities planned for the Centre should be entrusted to 'an Italian family' rather than the usual institutional caterers, but with no success.

The Port Health Committee Chairman told Common Council that new crematoria at the City's Manor Park Cemetery would shortly become operational, making the City's facilities the most advanced in Europe.

Never a dull moment!

9

AN EARLY THREAT TO BARTS, OPENING OF THE MUSEUM OF LONDON AND WE ENTERTAIN THE QUEEN

We went into 1977 with three more Barbican residents having been elected to Common Council – John Wooldridge, Michael Scrivener and Tom Fripp. That left just Derek Balls as the sole surviving non-resident for Cripplegate Ward. We had lost Budge Brooks (who happily returned to us in 1979), Wallis Hunt, who decided not to stand again after his distinguished record on Common Council, and Harold Titchener, who retired for health reasons.

The old and new members were in good voice at Common Council meetings speaking on a variety of topics – the right of people to be married by registrar in the City rather than having to go to Islington; the considerable cost of putting up and taking down the awning over the Guildhall porch (it eventually became a permanent – and attractive – feature); the rates (of course!); Barbican problems; and conservation.

All in all it was an extraordinarily busy year for all at Guildhall. The City's first development plan, a planning blueprint for future years, was under way; new conservation areas were being considered, Tower Bridge was given a major cleaning and steps taken to restrict the amount of lorry traffic using it.

John Packard, chairman of the Port Health Committee reported on an outbreak of food poisoning traced back to cockles from the Thames Estuary and on a brighter note told us there was an upturn of trade in the London docks with more examinations of food imports by the City's inspectors.

A curiosity at that time was a Corporation proposal to provide stress counselling for the commuters arriving daily in the City – little did anyone foresee the far greater stresses of twenty years or so later! In the Corporation's 2,300 council flats, spread across its estates in Brixton, Southwark and Holloway, tenants were being encouraged to take in lodgers to help ease London's housing shortage.

Plans for the redevelopment of Spitalfields Market (still, of course, on its old site in Spitalfields just outside the City) were shelved – lack of money – as was the move of the fish market away from Billingsgate. Shortage of cash also led to a cutback in book purchases for the City's three libraries.

At Portland House in Basinghall Street, a million-pound refurbishment was completed and tenants were being sought to swell the funds of 'City's Cash', the special fund used to finance the City's schools and open spaces such as Epping Forest.

At the Barbican Centre work was progressing on the large (possibly over-large) theatre being purpose-built for the Royal Shakespeare Company, a theatre which the RSC would eventually abandon after the many millions of pounds subsidy poured into it by the Corporation. A concert hall was being created for 'a major national orchestra' – although at that time it had not yet been decided that the Barbican would become the home for the splendidly successful London Symphony Orchestra.

Stirrings of racial unrest were experienced in London at that time and some members of the City Police, called in to help the Met during violence in Lewisham, were injured.

The *London Evening News* on 20 January 1977 reported a warning of plans to move St Bartholomew's Hospital out of the City:

> Mr Douglas Woodward, a member of the Court of Common Council, claimed the government proposed to divert resources away from the teaching hospital and to resite it. He urged a plea should be made to the Secretary of State. Alderman Allan Davis, then Chairman of the City's Health Committee, agreed that it would not only harm London but the country as a whole.

Here was a first dire warning of things to come when, in the 1990s, misguided politicians would propose the destruction of one of the world's greatest hospitals. More of that later.

There were some happier moments with the opening of the splendid Museum of London perched over the traffic roundabout at the western end of London Wall. It combined the holdings of the old Guildhall Museum and those of the London Museum at Lancaster House and would be funded by the government, the Corporation and the GLC (until its demise).

The most joyous occasion of 1977 was the Queen's Silver Jubilee visit to St Paul's for a thanksgiving service after which she and Prince Philip walked down Cheapside to the Guildhall for a celebration luncheon.

The Queen, Prince Philip and other members of the Royal Family have always been as highly regarded in the City as they deserved to be and our feelings of admiration and affection are clearly appreciated. Later, at a dark time, the Queen chose to make her 'annus horribilis' speech during a banquet in her honour at Guildhall where she knew there would be a particularly sympathetic audience. Again, it was at a dinner of the Planning Committee in Mansion House that Prince Charles chose to express his feelings about modern architecture. Princess Anne is a frequent visitor as a member of livery companies, particularly those with riding connections.

When, at the request of government, the City entertains visiting dignitaries at Guildhall banquets, members of the Royal Family are invariably in attendance – Princess Alexandra and Sir Angus Ogilvy, the Duke and Duchess of Kent and, in more recent times, the Duke and Duchess of Gloucester are welcomed by the Lord Mayor on their arrival at Guildhall just ahead of the chief guest that night.

These great occasions are underpinned by the City's special relationships with the Foreign and Commonwealth Office and especially with Buckingham Palace, the City Remembrancer being the important link man.

During my time on the Court of Common Council there were four men who fulfilled the duties of this high office with great flair, none more so than the 6 ft 4 Adrian Barnes who held the position from 1986 to 2003 and with whom I was later to work closely on a number of events.

The next chapter will look at the City's role as special provider of entertainment on behalf of government and Palace.

10

THE 'GLITTERING OCCASIONS' – AND ONE OR TWO WHICH GLITTERED LESS!

The City is renowned for the splendour of its hospitality and certainly in past centuries the exemplar of great dining and wining was a 'Mansion House Banquet'.

The tradition has survived although by my day the number of courses served had shrunk to a mere four or five and although the Lord Mayor's home, the Mansion House, remains a centre for entertaining, the really big occasions are at the Guildhall which can accommodate over 700 against the 340 of Mansion House.

Mansion House is the venue for the banquets given every year to the diplomatic corps, the judges, the bishops, the bankers, the arts and the livery companies. They were (and still largely are) white tie affairs with the men who have them sporting their medals and the ladies their tiaras. Alas the bankers' dinner was downgraded when Mr Brown, then Chancellor of the Exchequer, insisted on wearing his blue suit.

During my twenty-five years on Common Council I think that every ruling European monarch, every notable president worldwide and other heads of state came to be entertained in Guildhall at truly glittering occasions, all at the behest of the government of the day, many being guests of the Queen and staying at Buckingham Palace.

The routine was for Her Majesty to give a welcoming banquet on the Tuesday of their visit, for the City to entertain them on the Wednesday, and for the visitor to return hospitality at his embassy (if large enough) or one of the London hotels, Claridges or the Park Lane being the usual choice.

The Guildhall arrangements were conducted with the greatest precision under the tight supervision of the Remembrancer. The arrangements began many weeks, sometimes months, before, as soon as dates had been finalised between the Foreign Office and the visiting head of state.

A reception committee numbering thirty members, one for each City ward plus Aldermen and Chief Commoner, would be nominated on a rota system by the Town Clerk in Common Council and it was they, guided by the Remembrancer, who would make all the detailed arrangements for the big night. There was invariably keen competition among the members as to which should be elected Chairman. There was competition, also, to be nominated as a member of the small subcommittee entrusted to attend the tasting of the various dishes, champagnes and other wines suggested by the chosen caterer and thus to decide on the final menu.

Among the small group of caterers on the Guildhall approved list the competition to 'win' one of these banquets was equally keen. In my earlier years, Ring & Brymer and Payne & Gunter were the two firms in most frequent contest, the chairman of the reception committees knowing that either of them was a 'safe pair of hands' for an event where some 700 people were likely to be invited and at which absolutely nothing could be allowed to go even slightly wrong. In more recent times the list of caterers has changed and grown somewhat larger, chairmen being encouraged to try out new talent.

Of course, catering was only one – if the most important – requirement. There was the careful wording of an address of welcome that on the night would be read out by the Recorder of London. There was the design of a suitably impressive menu card, preparation of the complex table plan, engagement of the State trumpeters to sound the fanfares announcing each of the toasts, and the appointment of the toast-master to announce the guests (invariably Bernard Sullivan who could be implicitly trusted to get his tongue round the most difficult of foreign names).

On the morning of the great day, at 8 a.m., a dress rehearsal would take place in the Old Library at Guildhall, the place where guests would later be received by the Lord Mayor. In attendance would be the Remembrancer and his team, the Lord Mayor and Lady Mayoress, Sheriffs and their ladies, Swordbearer and Mace Bearer (using umbrellas at the rehearsal in place of sword and mace), chairman of the reception committee and the Chief Commoner who had moved the resolution long before in Common Council that such and such should be entertained.

Every step in the ceremony that would take place that evening was carefully rehearsed so that all the major Corporation players would know exactly where they would be and what they would have to do.

At 7 p.m. the proceedings would start. The Lord Mayor and Lady Mayoress, now in their finery, would take their places on the dais in the Old Library, ready to receive the earliest guests. Members of the Court of Common Council in their gowns of mazarine blue and wearing white kid gloves, were already seated with their ladies. The military band would strike up, and the Chairman of the Reception Committee would march down the aisle to be received by the Lord Mayor before going off to his duties. Members of the Reception Committee, armed with their wands of office, would be stationed at strategic points to usher the guests to their places. The reception would start with the most important of them processing down the centre aisle of the Old Library to be welcomed by the Lord Mayor and seated on the dais behind him. At the appointed moment the Lord Mayor, Lady Mayoress and their attendants would process out to wait on the Guildhall porch, first for the Royals on duty that night, and then for the head of state himself.

Back they all came in procession, the visitor's national anthem played (sometimes at great length), the address of welcome read in sonorous tones by the Recorder of London and then presented to the visitor in a silver casket. The Chairman of the Reception Committee, the Chief Commoner, Senior Aldermen and the Sheriffs would be presented to the king or president. At last the Remembrancer would announce that 'Dinner is about to be served', at which most guests would be shepherded into Great Hall while some of the more privileged would assemble in the nearby Print Room for a pre-banquet glass of champagne. Then the banquet itself, the toasts and speeches – sometimes in English, often in another tongue with translations, set before each guest.

These were truly glittering occasions and as members of Common Council we felt ourselves greatly privileged to be part of such splendid entertainment, especially when the chief guest was a popular European king or queen or, say, the United States or French president.

My first moment of glory was when I found myself elected Chairman of the Reception Committee for the banquet in honour of King Fahd of Saudi Arabia when after the formal presentation to him at the reception in the Old Library one had the chance of talking to him just before dinner in the Print Room as well as to that most agreeable Royal, the Duke of Gloucester, who, with the Duchess, was in attendance that night. My wife, Ann, enjoyed herself as much as I did and after the conclusion of the banquet we were both on the Guildhall porch with the Lord Mayor to wave farewell to the king.

Of course, not every one of our visiting dignitaries was of the same high calibre. In hindsight, it was certainly not a good idea to have made much of Ceauşescu, the Romanian president (or dictator), as a guest in Guildhall (still less to have inflicted him on Her Majesty at the Palace). Just occasionally our chief guest was late in arriving and the cause of considerable nail-biting on the part of the Remembrancer. There was no excuse for the King of Morocco to be half an hour late, bearing in mind the squad of police motorcyclists ready to deliver him to Guildhall at the prescribed time! The very worst of our heads of state visitors, though, was almost certainly President Mobutu of Zaire and his entourage who, in their high-buttoned jackets and dark glasses, reminded Ann and me of Haiti's *Tonton Macoutes*.

That night, when we sat down to dinner in the Great Hall, our Zaire neighbour, an engaging young man, brought in with him a long wooden box which he stashed under the table. I asked him what his job was (head of security complete with guns, perhaps).

'Je suis le chef du protocol,' he told us. To keep the conversation going Ann said, 'Ask him if he's married.' I did and he replied *'Non, mais j'ai une concubine.'*

'Only one?' I asked.

'Ah, vous comprenez que je suis encore jeune!'

One up to Zaire.

Clearly this invitation was certainly a mistake on the part of the Foreign Office – particularly when one later heard of the damage caused by the visitors at the Palace where they were staying. In a later chapter I will refer to another less than happy occasion involving Robert Mugabe.

Going back to our involvement with King Fahd, I should mention that his return banquet was at Claridges to which Ann and I had invitations. Unlike Guildhall the night before, this occasion was 'dry', with water or orange juice the only liquids available to accompany what seemed to us a rather indifferent dinner. Later over coffee we were with one of the young Saudi princes who told us that we should have joined him earlier in his suite for a 'snifter' of something stronger than orange juice!

11

WE ACT TO STOP DESTRUCTION OF THE CITY'S OLDER BUILDINGS

There was much activity on the planning front during 1978 with a great variety of cases coming before Common Council. A simple enough change of use from retail to offices on the ground floor of Bevis Marks House was opposed on the grounds that there was already a shortage of shops in the City. We had a proposal that the church of St Botolph, Aldersgate, should become an ecclesiastical museum but (no surprise this) that the adjoining Postman's Park must remain an open space. Permission was granted for an antiques market in Cutler Street, though nothing came of this. A new Barbican station building with shops adjoining and offices above was agreed. A first proposal for a floating heliport on the Thames was roundly rejected after powerful speeches against from members of riverside wards. There would be other attempts to land helicopters in the City's stretch of the river but all failed.

The biggest of the planning proposals recommended by the Planning Committee – which Common Council ill-advisedly approved – was that Touche Remnant should be allowed to redevelop the site of the Mermaid Theatre at Puddle Dock, a replacement theatre being submerged into the ugly office development still there. This second Mermaid never took off as a theatre, alas, Bernard Miles no longer being involved.

The Corporation was still hard up and the Guildhall Art Gallery (a very utilitarian temporary structure put up after the war damage at Guildhall) was to be closed for a year as an economy measure. Of course it was the rates money that was short and happily money was available in the City's private funds to create a 'Midsummer Prize' of £1,500 to recognise achievement in the arts which the Lord Mayor would present at his Midsummer Banquet in the Mansion House.

Lord Mayor Peter Vanneck, after an official visit to France, proposed that there should be an annual 'Paris Lecture' on a subject of mutual interest to both countries, the first lecture to be given at the City University's Centre of Banking and International Finance by a Frenchman nominated by the Mayor of Paris – an interesting idea that did not long survive, however.

An idea that has endured was that a charitable trust be set up for the City of London School to provide bursaries for pupils unable for financial reasons to continue at the school or, having been accepted, could not take up their places.

Caroline Gordon who, in a previous existence, had, as a member of the male sex, fathered two boys, was elected as a new Cripplegate member at the end of 1978, encouraged to do so by Brigadier John Packard. Our Ward Deputies now were Wilfrid Dewhirst and Derek Balls.

Conservation Award Set Up

For me the most notable event of 1978 was the establishment of the City Heritage Award to encourage the saving and refurbishment of worthwhile old City buildings in place of their destruction and total redevelopment – the fate of all too many Victorian buildings which had survived wartime bombing.

Such an award had long been in the mind of the City Heritage Society but we first had to have additional, particularly financial, backing. We found the ideal partner for this enterprise in the Worshipful Company of Painter-Stainers, the broker being our Cripplegate Alderman, Allan Davis, a liveryman of that company.

The second of our City Heritage Awards – for Whitbread's Porter Tun Room – with Lord Mayor Kenneth Cork

The launch party took place in April 1978 at Painters'
Hall in Little Trinity Lane with speeches by the Master
(former Lord Mayor Sir Ralph Perring) and me. We
had a surprisingly good press – for the City of London
to be embarking on a conservation project was news
indeed – and with considerable alacrity we had our
first Award in October. The Lord Mayor, Sir Peter
Vanneck, had accepted an invitation to do the honours
on that drizzling October morning and we made our
speeches outside the chosen winner, a modest little
surveyors' office in Newbury Street, St
Bartholomew's. The building itself was too small to
hold the celebration party and so we all trooped off to
drink champagne at Painters' Hall. I have to say that
ever since then the Award recipients (quite accidentally
of course) have tended to be bigger buildings with
adequate space for the fifty or so participants to
celebrate – and the willingness to foot the bill for
champagne themselves!

Every year up till the present time we have been
fortunate in having the Lord Mayor of the day to
present these awards for outstanding excellence in
building conservation and the commemorative bronze
plaques are to be seen on buildings throughout the
Square Mile, including some very grand ones like the
Royal Exchange, Bank of England and Mansion
House, as well as more modest examples of successful
refurbishment and renewal.

There is no doubt that the City Heritage Awards
have played an important part in persuading owners of
buildings, developers and architects, to seriously
consider the refurbishment option as against

redevelopment, and they have certainly helped maintain the character of such areas as Smithfield. Our award was the first of its kind in Britain and has since been extensively imitated – another first for the City!

12

DEATH KNELL FOR THE FUR TRADE AND A NEW LLOYD'S PROPOSED

Early 1979, the eve of Margaret Thatcher's arrival at the forefront of the political scene.

Here in the City (as elsewhere) things were not all that bright. The weather did not help. The Corporation was under attack that freezing January for not having gritted the City streets and clearing them of ice and snow. 'The City cleansing department's road gangs must have stayed in bed nursing their New Year hangovers' moaned a letter writer in the *City Recorder* newspaper.

Strikes were the order of the day, with the railways specially affected. There were stories in the papers that because of these strikes, affecting commuting into the City, firms were upping sticks and locating elsewhere. Even Corporation dustmen had been on strike seeking a bigger pay-rise. At Bart's Hospital, waiting lists for admissions topped 3,000.

In Common Council, Alderman Sir Edward Howard was again fulminating against ever-rising costs for the Barbican Arts Centre, up from the original £16 million budget to £80 million. The final bill would rise to £150 million. George Vine, former Chairman of the

Barbican Committee retorted that it was Sir Edward's fault because of the delays his arguments had caused. A well-known Barbican resident and financial journalist, S W Alexander, wrote to the *City Recorder* supporting Sir Edward: 'The Court of Common Council, like national government, is financially irresponsible and profligate with peoples' money.'

Bloody but fairly unbowed the Corporation soldiered on. In Common Council we approved plans for Tower Bridge to become an exhibition centre and tourist attraction. In the course of that debate I suggested that it should contain a record of the Bridge's history since its opening by Queen Victoria – and all this came to pass with considerable success.

Over at the still very unfinished Barbican Centre, Henry Wrong, who had been appointed Director years earlier, led players from the London Symphony Orchestra (in hard hats) on a tour of what would one day become their London home.

George Cunningham, the Labour MP for South Islington, said in the local newspaper that wealthy Barbican residents paid too little rent and that the City Corporation should charge them more, using the proceeds to subsidise Islington tenants on the nearby Golden Lane Estate.

Golden Lane residents had their own ideas, and some years later were to petition to leave Islington and be incorporated within the City of London – a development which also came to pass to the satisfaction of all concerned.

The fairly constant allegations as to the 'wealth' of Barbican residents spurred the Barbican Association to carry out a survey to identify the occupations of these rich residents and we discovered a great mixture including the odd factory worker and some nurses.

In any event life would soon be transformed for Barbican tenants whose flats could up to that time only be rented. After much debate and discussion with government housing ministers we had the first assurances in Common Council that Barbican would be included in Mrs Thatcher's new 'Right to Buy' legislation.

End of the Fur Trade in Sight

Down in the Garlick Hill and Skinners Lane area of the City, off Upper Thames Street, redolent with its very special smell of the long-established fur trade, there were signs that this historic trade would soon be coming to an end – sad not only for the fur traders but because it would mean the loss of another of the City's few remaining industrial activities. Later would come the loss of an even larger trade activity, the newspaper and printing industry, which for so long had been City-based in Fleet Street and its surrounding streets and alleys. Thus the City, which once had thrived on the diversity of its business life, would become almost entirely reliant on its banking, insurance, dealing and related financial activities – happily all very strong but of course all too vulnerable to the kind of economic setbacks which occur from time to time. This was the reason why in the City Heritage Society we had always urged the retention of the meat market at Smithfield, the enhancement of medical activity based on Bart's

Hospital and any other activity to maintain some diversity in the City's life – not least, of course, an enlargement of its housing stock.

In that regard we regretted that the Old Deanery (erected in 1670) opposite St Paul's – no longer, it seemed, needed by the Church authorities – would be turned into offices. At least the building, then in a rather sorry state, would be saved from dereliction. Years later we would welcome its return as a home for the Bishop of London, Richard Chartres, who had a proper appreciation of its rightful use.

In 1979 came the edict that Aldermen would have to retire on reaching the age of seventy and it was Christopher Collett, elected as the new Alderman for the ward of Broad Street, who was the first to be appointed under this new rule.

A New Lloyd's Proposed

There was one other planning event that year which would have wide repercussions and that was the proposal for a new and spectacular building for the Lloyd's insurance market in Leadenhall Street.

City Heritage had been invited to look at the plans and Richard Rogers and the Lloyd's Chairman welcomed seventy of us there one summer evening to see what Rogers was proposing to do. Our reaction was that the drawings showed promise and that in general we were supportive. (We should have taken warning from the Pompidou Centre!) This was City Heritage's almost only mistake over the years, and most of us would be appalled at the eventual result. It certainly taught us a lesson never to be persuaded by an architect's drawings or model – often they are apparent pussy cats which when built turn into monsters.

Soon after our visit to Lloyd's, when the planning application, approved by the Planning Committee, came to Common Council, Tony Bull, then a Councilman, later an Alderman, bitterly and quite rightly attacked the Rogers design which he described as a cross between a Blackpool helter-skelter and an Emett building; but with scant support from others the new Lloyd's got the Council's go-ahead. Here was the beginning of the indication to architects and developers that, in future years, the City's traditional way of building in stone and brick with the emphasis on classical style could safely be broached. With this new structure, soon to be likened to the oil well of Leadenhall Street, there would be a clear signal that architecturally in the City 'anything goes'. Happily, for a good many years, developers would not be taking too much advantage of this new freedom.

At the Lord Mayor's Banquet in November, Sir Peter Gadsden welcomed as his chief guest that night our new prime minister. Never before (at least not since the days of Winston Churchill) had there been such a rapturous reception as Margaret Thatcher and her husband received from the 720 people present as they walked down the aisle in the Old Library; and then later, after her speech in the Great Hall, came the longest standing ovation ever afforded a prime minister – when such things were not as commonplace as they are today.

13

THE DONALD SILK AFFAIR

In July 1979 Donald Silk, one of our colleagues on Cripplegate Ward, had decided to have a go at becoming the Alderman for Aldersgate where Sir Gilbert Inglefield, former Lord Mayor, had recently retired. The other contestant was Frank McWilliams, also a Barbican resident and currently the Chairman of the Barbican Association of residents. Aldersgate and Cripplegate were the two wards which between them took in all the flats and houses on the Barbican Estate. Silk defeated McWilliams and thus the way seemed open to his becoming Alderman – with, in the fullness of time, the progression towards becoming Aldermanic Sheriff and ultimately Lord Mayor.

A month later, in August, the Court of Aldermen vetoed his election and thus began a twelve-month saga, the echoes from which were to resound around the City – and far further afield – for many a day.

I had first met Donald a few years earlier when I was canvassing for votes on my own behalf as a Common Councilman. Calling at his house in the Postern I was invited in to meet a collection of well-known Labour faces (Tom Driberg was one – I've forgotten who the others were) and given a large whisky while Donald's coterie plied me with questions all amounting to friendly contempt for the City's 'lack of democracy'. They were astonishingly ignorant of how the City worked and clearly taken aback when I pointed out that unlike the neighbouring boroughs our councillors had to face the electorate annually (only too true for Cripplegate).

'But how can you possibly call yourselves democratic without your members belonging to a political party?' was a central question. The idea of 185 independents was beyond their understanding. Obviously we were a weird bunch.

But Donald at least must have been impressed for not only did he give me his vote but not long afterwards stood as a candidate himself, and was duly elected for Cripplegate.

Most of us liked him. He had qualified as a solicitor, was a successful businessman, had plenty to say for himself, and did not appear to take life too seriously. His marriage at an earlier time to the tennis star Angela Buxton also spoke in his favour. But looking at the serving Aldermen and the part played by the Lord Mayor I really could not visualise him fitting comfortably in that role. At the end of 1979 he appealed in the High Court which upheld the Court of Aldermen's right of veto.

However, when in February 1980 a further aldermanic election was called in Aldersgate, he stood once more against Frank McWilliams and a third candidate, Common Councilman David Shalit. Silk was elected with an increased majority, the result announced in a crowded Ironmongers' Hall by Lord Mayor Sir Peter Gadsden who left a City dinner to preside, the press being present in force.

In March, the Court of Aldermen again turned Silk down having listened to but not being convinced by his twenty-five-minute speech in which he pointed out all the reasons why they should accept him. He said he was considering his next step – possibly an appeal to the European Court of Justice.

In the event, Silk settled for yet another attempt in the third aldermanic election which was held on 30 April 1980 and on this occasion Frank McWilliams won a twelve-vote majority in an election with an extraordinarily high turnout, 570 votes being cast.

The Court of Aldermen confirmed in June that McWilliams would be the new Alderman for the Ward of Aldersgate. And thus the Donald Silk affair came at last to an end, although it had certainly brought about much undesirable publicity for the City and its after-effects would linger.

Caroline Gordon, another of our Cripplegate colleagues, wrote in the *City Recorder* defending the Court of Aldermen's decision, pointing out that in an aldermanic election the Ward electorate had the right to submit a name to the Court but it was the Court's prerogative, as laid down by the House of Lords in 1839, to veto that person if they saw fit to do so.

Colin Dyer, Chief Commoner in 1980, said in a speech that it was right for the City to maintain its separate government responsibilities not just because of its historic traditions but to look after its special needs as an international financial centre. At the same time he expressed his strong belief in the aldermanic system to ensure the right choice of the person to be Lord Mayor.

Twenty years later, the Court of Aldermen would lose their power of veto over incoming Aldermen. There has been a most unfortunate result with people who have already served as Aldermen for several years finding that their progression towards becoming Sheriff is permanently blocked because the Court of Aldermen, rather late in the day, decide that they are unacceptable as future Lord Mayors. Thus the supply of suitable candidates for the office of Lord Mayor is severely diminished. That power of veto, right at the start, really had much to recommend it! Other moves at Guildhall more recently have added to these aldermanic problems.

Argument Over City Loos

Much else was happening in the City during 1980. To ease expenditure the Corporation proposed to shut down five of its public lavatories – the saving to accrue from the wages of the five attendants. There was opposition in the Court of Common Council from Edward Clements about the closure of the loo at the junction of Fleet Street and Fetter Lane. He said that if it was shut people would use the alleys in his Ward of Farringdon Without. Why not employ just one or two 'roving attendants' to keep an eye on all five? Not an idea the Court approved, however.

Trying to Pedestrianise Fleet Street and Some Good News for Conservation

With the start of the exodus from Fleet Street of a few newspapers there was a rather odd move by some

Guildhall officers and members to encourage acceleration of this process and thus allow Fleet Street itself, one of the busiest of City routes, to be pedestrianised. The 'traffic-stoppers' had clearly forgotten an earlier move to close Ludgate Hill to vehicles, a very unpopular and a silly idea that quickly caused traffic chaos. There were always a few who were keen to restrict vehicles from City streets but happily we held them at bay for a good many years by making fun of their projects to close streets or introduce complicated one-way systems. Eventually, though, their dream came to be realised after the 1993 IRA bomb in Bishopsgate which opened the way for the City's 'ring of steel' and associated road closures.

Just around the corner from Fleet Street a scheme for a big office development on the site of the old *Evening Standard* offices was turned down by the Planning Committee as being too massive and over-dominant. This year of 1980 indeed promised well for conservation.

Developers with their eye on the Old Billingsgate fish market building (part of the City's own property holdings) had a shock when Michael Heseltine, without a doubt one of the best ever Secretaries of State for the Environment, proposed to 'list' the splendid Victorian building designed in 1874–8 by Sir Horace Jones, the City Architect and Surveyor. It was not only the property developers who were put out – the Chairman of the Billingsgate Committee, Peter Rigby, saw the prospects for a big cash purchase receding, money he needed to help finance the move of the market to its new location in the Docks. He said somewhat bitterly that the government should now be made to foot the bill.

However, the City Lands Committee (which oversees the Corporation's property portfolio) responded more positively to the listing and declared that Billingsgate would not be sold off but should be sensitively refurbished for mixed use as offices, flats and shops. This worthy objective never came off, alas, but old Billingsgate has served various useful purposes though it is still looking for a long-term occupant even today.

Michael Heseltine decided on another listing – that of the former Guildhall School of Music and Drama in John Carpenter Street, another splendid example of Victoriana, by Sir Horace Jones, the facades of which still stand.

Little wonder, perhaps, that towards the close of 1980 a furious attack on conservation was launched by Chief Commoner Colin Dyer. The occasion was a debate in Common Council where Planning Chairman, the admirable Norman Harding, proposed that Garlick Hill should become the City's tenth 'conservation area'. Dyer said that conservation policies threatened the City with 'creeping paralysis' and that it would become just 'one big museum'. My comment in the Court that day was that where a conservation area was introduced it certainly did not mean that buildings within it could never be replaced, only to safeguard them against inappropriate or ugly development. The proposal was carried with overwhelming approval. Indeed, a good year for conservation.

Warning to Diplomats

Lord Mayor Sir Peter Gadsden told guests at the banquet for the diplomatic corps in the Mansion House that diplomats, once treated with great respect, were now at serious risk of being assassinated or taken hostage (as long ago as 1980!).

Like all our Lord Mayors he travelled widely, and not just in his year of office. He told us in his speech that every time he had ever gone abroad he had brought back for his wife, Belinda, (she and Peter were our neighbours in the Barbican) a gold charm from the country he was visiting. 'Tonight she is wearing a bracelet which has on it forty-five such charms, the first dating from 1952.'

That year the Fabian Society came up with one of its quainter ideas – that the City and much of Westminster, Camden, Islington, Lambeth and Tower Hamlets should be gobbled up in what they called a new 'Superborough' for central London. The City had little need to comment on this abolition threat since the other boroughs (mostly Labour controlled) did all the protesting necessary to scupper this silly idea.

The City's 'beadles' – one from every ward – (they attended their Aldermen on civic occasions) together with those attached to livery companies, had their own rather more sensible view, and at their annual City dinner the Chairman of the Beadles said it was high time the City's critics copied the Corporation's method of government instead of seeking to destroy it.

Queen Mother in the City

In July, the Queen Mother arrived in the Port of London on the Royal Yacht Britannia to attend her eightieth birthday celebration service at St Paul's, driving through the City in an open landau with Prince Charles at her side, to be greeted on the cathedral steps by the Lord Mayor.

Over the centuries Guildhall had its Keeper who was responsible in my day for looking after the whole complex of buildings and whose many other duties included the induction of new members into Common Council, making the arrangements for Council meetings and taking care of the many dinners and other events which took place in Guildhall. It all worked beautifully under Hallkeeper Alan Marshall and when he retired after thirty-seven years working for the Corporation, his successor, John Lucioni carried on in like manner, living with his wife 'over the shop' in a top flat in the new Guildhall west wing. Such a pity that the Keeper's department was scrapped in the year 2000 – an early casualty of the Corporation's streamlining programme.

Donald Silk gave up his aldermanic dreams and rejoined his old pals in Cripplegate. Paul Newall, an investment banker, easily won a by-election to join us too – a somewhat surprising accomplishment for a non-resident but Paul, soon himself to embark on an aldermanic career (Lord Mayor 1993–4), had the personality and the will to achieve whatever he set his mind to.

14

ROYAL WEDDING AND ANOTHER LABOUR ATTACK REBUFFED

The year 1981 was of course dominated here in the City – as everywhere else – by the marriage that summer in St Paul's Cathedral of Prince Charles and Lady Diana Spencer and, ill-fated as it was destined to be, it brought much joy and colour to the London scene in the weeks beforehand and on the day itself.

The crowds had staked out their places along the processional route many hours earlier and on the evening before, Ludgate Hill was already the scene of festivities with, among the sleeping bags, quite a few picnic tables whose occupants, in dinner jackets and long dresses, were already sipping champagne.

Some of the more senior members of the Court of Common Council were to join the Lord Mayor and Lady Mayoress inside St Paul's. Ann and I also did well with seats on the balcony of Juxon House opposite sharing, the space with the world's television teams and some interesting neighbours including actresses Hermione Gingold and Ann Clements. The service was broadcast to us, and just before it ended when Kiri Te Kanawa was in full song, we made our way back to friends in the Barbican for our own champagne celebration.

A Small Scandal

There was much else that year to occupy the City before and after the wedding.

In Cripplegate Ward we had elected three new residents to serve on Common Council, one of whom, our friend John Barker, unlike so many others who tended to come on and go off quite quickly, would stay the course right up to the present time. Michael Cassidy, elected for the neighbouring Ward of Aldersgate, was another to stay the course and to become a noted Chairman of both the Planning and Policy Committees. In 1981 he was still very much a spokesman for Barbican residents, arguing that the prices being set by the Corporation for its Barbican flats at between £26,000 and £300,000 were too high and certainly higher than many of the existing tenants could afford to buy.

We had a bit of a scandal in that some thirty of the postal votes cast in the previous December election were declared to be invalid. The problem was that some partners in Coopers & Lybrand, which had offices in two different parts of the City – Farringdon Within and Cripplegate – had inadvertently voted in both.

We Give Thanks

In May, Alfred Dubs, the Labour MP for Battersea South, put down a motion in the Commons calling for abolition of the Corporation of London as a local government unit and for its resources (all that lovely 'City's Cash') and its functions to be transferred to 'one or more adjacent boroughs'. He said in his speech, 'I want the City to be the same as the rest of London', although he kindly added that the Lord Mayor could continue his role, with the City's ancient traditions becoming a tourist attraction.

This latest bit of envy and malice was roundly defeated in the House and later that month I put down my motion in Common Council thanking the 236 Members of Parliament (the Conservatives of course) who had voted against Dubs. Joe Brown, formerly a leading Tory light on the GLC, seconded my motion.

The *City Recorder* newspaper reported thus:

Mr C D Woodward – 'I would say to Mr Dubs that we residents in the City are perfectly happy with the kind of democracy we have. We do not want to be taken over by you or any of the neighbouring big boroughs […] We have to accept as a fact though that one political party is determined to do away with us.'

Mr B J Brown, the Chief Commoner – 'We have cleared the air at least for a short while […] Mr Dubs forgot to mention that City elections are held annually whereas in the rest of the country it is every four years.'

But some members of the Court did not approve – 'We should not be dragged into politics in this way […] We are a non-political organisation.'

Happily my motion was overwhelmingly carried.

This year the City went in for its own beauty contest, Lord Mayor Ronnie Gardner-Thorpe inaugurating 'Miss City Girl 1981' in April. It was all quite select with the candidates dressed first in day clothes and then evening dress – no swimsuits in the City! The winner, twenty-year-old Anita Hanson, and the two runners-up, were feted in the Mansion House in July.

A proposal to close two of the City's four public libraries (to save money) proved very unpopular with 10,000 people signing a petition to keep the Cannon Street Library open and Barbican residents up in arms against the threatened closure of the Cripplegate Library until a new one opened in the Barbican Centre. Sir Kenneth Cork, former Lord Mayor, said in Common Council that the library closures made the Corporation look 'mean and silly'. While money was short for other City activities we were told that the cost of the Arts Centre (originally estimated at £16 million) had soared to £136 million.

Dr James Cope, one of the Councilmen for Farringdon Without Ward, told Common Council that every time someone sat down in the Arts Centre's new theatre it would cost City ratepayers £12 in subsidy. 'Pericles had ensured that the Athenian poor were subsidised to go to the theatre,' he said. 'We are doing it for other than the poor and in surroundings very different to the Acropolis!'

Dancing in the Crypt

We had a new, rather young, Lord Mayor in Christopher Leaver with an even younger wife and two daughters, one aged four, the other six months. Unusually, the Mansion House would echo to children's voices.

At the banquet that November the youthfulness of the Lord Mayor and Lady Mayoress was signalled by a dance in the east crypt after the conclusion of the dinner and speeches upstairs. Ann had her first experience of dancing with one of the pikemen, complete with breastplate and sword, while I enjoyed dancing with Shirley, the wife of the City's Commissioner of Police, the admirable Jim Page.

Robert Runcie, the Archbishop of Canterbury, and Anna Neagle, the actress, were admitted as Freemen of the City of London in two (quite separate) ceremonies but with each of the two new Freemen widely acclaimed.

In June, the Queen came to the City to open the first of the City's skyscraper office buildings – Seifert's 600-foot Natwest Tower. It had long been on the stocks and at that time none of us dreamt that twenty years later it would become the excuse for a cluster of surrounding towers that would change the City's skyline.

There was a surprising new head of the GLC in 1981, Mr K Livingstone, whose highly political agenda and money-spending schemes would very shortly cause consternation among London's ratepayers.

The Chairman of our Finance Committee announced swingeing rates increases in the City where we collected almost £300 million of which only a quarter went for the City's own needs. Big City firms were facing rates bills of £500,000 and for residents there was a 40% supplementary rate levied by the GLC and ILEA. For me it was very much back to rates campaigning – and a further opportunity to have a go at the GLC/ILEA juggernaut.

15

INTO TOP GEAR ON RATES AND WE SET UP THE CITY OF LONDON RATEPAYERS' ASSOCIATION

From autumn 1981 into the spring of 1982, we were pulling out all the stops to combat the rates menace affecting the City.

In October 1981 more than 300 residents in Barbican and other parts of the City met once again in the City of London Girls' School to protest about the 40% supplementary rate levied by the GLC and ILEA when residents unanimously agreed to petition the Secretary of State for the Environment, Michael Heseltine.

> We the undersigned, residents in the City of London, draw to your attention the increasingly onerous rates burden under which we suffer and which is almost entirely the result of the precepts levied by the GLC and ILEA.
>
> We recognise that ratepayers throughout Greater London are suffering in like manner, but the special circumstances of the City with its high rateable values result in the burden being even heavier here.
>
> We therefore petition you to alleviate the burden on ratepayers in the City by putting a ceiling on the demands of the preceptory authorities.

Over the next few days the petition would be signed by many hundreds of City residents from the Temple to Queen's Quay and the Barbican.

In my speech at the Girls' School, I said that the present situation, while bad enough, would be even worse in 1982 when the GLC promised a further enormous increase in their levy. 'So far as I can make out the GLC themselves have not the slightest idea just how much their policies are going to cost the rest of us. It's a good thing the City's debtors' prisons are no longer functioning otherwise they'd be full of City residents who cannot afford to pay the GLC rates.'

We had Patrick Roney, Chairman of the City Corporation's Finance Committee, with us on the platform that evening who cried: 'The Corporation must not fear to oppose GLC policies which are based on blind prejudice and self-opinionated arrogance and which will culminate in the financial ruin of many City ratepayers large and small. I believe the Corporation's voice must be loud and clear on behalf of itself and its ratepayers in seeking a return to reason and sanity.'

The petition with 1,127 signatures was shortly delivered to Peter Brooke, our always helpful Member of Parliament, and thence presented to Mr Heseltine. To Margaret Thatcher I wrote: 'At a public meeting City residents supported a call that we should also write to you to enlist your sympathy and to support the resolve of your government to control profligate spending by some local authorities. We wish you and the Secretary of State well in this endeavour.'

The government response was rapid with a letter

from Lord Bellwin, the Environment Minister, reporting: 'the House of Lords have held that the GLC's supplementary precept for 1981/1982 is illegal.' London boroughs were being advised to credit ratepayers who had paid the supplementary rates levy. For the future, local authorities powers to raise supplementary rates were to be abolished. The government had just published a Green Paper looking at possible alternatives to the domestic rating system 'which can give rise to unfairness and anomalies', said Lord Bellwin.

We were fortunate, of course, at this time to have a strong government in office which was only too willing to acknowledge the kind of problems to which we had drawn attention and although careful to avoid 'naming names' there is no doubt that the Prime Minister and her colleagues were far from enamoured with the antics of the GLC. Our particular contribution must, I am sure, have been a factor in their eventual decision to scrap the GLC.

But that decision was still in the future and meanwhile it seemed to me and others that we had to take further steps to protect our interests.

So it was that, in April 1982, we established the City of London Ratepayers Association with the objectives of curbing excessive rate rises in the City and the Greater London area as a whole, ensuring that ratepayers got value for their money, and to protect ratepayers' interests generally. It would collaborate with other bodies through the already active Federation of London Ratepayers' Associations.

An executive committee of five was formed: myself

as the Chairman; Stella Currie, Treasurer; Valerie Meixner, Secretary; Barbara Williamson, Membership Secretary; and George Newman. (There's not much romance attached to rates but not too long afterwards Barbara and George were to marry!). 'Budge' Brooks, a fellow Common Councilman, joined us later. Barbara Newman, as she became, was elected as a Common Councilman for Aldersgate Ward, and went on to great things, including being Chief Commoner in 1999.

Our manifesto made clear the particular targets in our sights:

> It appears to the Association that the major threat to City ratepayers is posed by the Greater London Council and Inner London Education Authority and it is in connection with the rate precepts of these authorities that the Association is proposing to direct its major activity [...] The Association considers that local government in Greater London is over-structured and overmanned and recommends radical reform with either abolition of the GLC tier or at least a drastic reduction in its size and functions [...] Education provision in inner London should either be taken over by central government or ILEA's functions should be shared among the inner London boroughs.

The Association rapidly attracted well over two hundred members, chiefly residents but a few business firms as well. It was to remain fully active over the next ten years even after our particular enemy, the GLC, had been disposed of.

I was not overly thrilled with the government's

Green Paper 'Alternatives to Domestic Rate', and wrote to Lord Bellwin to that effect in March (1982) and then again to suggest that abolition of the GLC would be the easiest and most effective way to curb excessive rates demands – at least so far as London was concerned.

Also that month in Common Council when Finance Committee Chairman Patrick Roney, introducing the City's budget for 1982/1983, had criticised GLC policies, I had this to say:

> While businesses have to save and scrimp County Hall totally ignores the facts of economic life, spending millions as though it were water. The GLC/ILEA precepts are utterly disgraceful and should not be accepted by the Court. We know that inflation is down by one whole point. A major reason was the withdrawal of the GLC's illegal supplementary rate. We can imagine what the new GLC rates – 22.5% up for commercial ratepayers – will do for inflation!

Later that year, following an open meeting for our members at the Museum of London, we sent a message of support to the London Boroughs Association which, under the chairmanship of Peter Bowness, had begun its own attempt to abolish the GLC.

The Association's first annual general meeting took place in January 1984 in the crypt of St Mary-le-Bow Church when we reported that membership had risen to 235 and noted that the government, in a recent White Paper, proposed that the GLC should be abolished and its functions transferred to the boroughs and the City Corporation. Writing to the Secretary of State at that time, I suggested that the City could usefully take on some of the GLC's functions for the benefit of London as a whole – an idea that was to come to fruition at a later date. Meanwhile the GLC and ILEA rates precepts had been capped by the government which meant that domestic rates in the City had at least been stabilised.

A year later, with legislation to abolish the GLC at an advanced stage, we told our members at the 1985 AGM how delighted we were that the government were pressing ahead with a measure for which we had agitated so long. In Guildhall, in March 1985, with the Finance Chairman forecasting substantial savings when services moved from the GLC to the boroughs, I said that City ratepayers would certainly expect to benefit from these savings. In September, I again wrote to the Secretary of State to voice our concern that under a new London Rate Equalisation Scheme the money the City would be called on to provide for the boroughs (as much as £120 million) could deprive City ratepayers of any such benefit. The lengthy reply included the promise: 'The government hopes that after abolition there will be significant savings.'

But any euphoria about the GLC's demise would soon be dissipated by new storm clouds gathering for the City's luckless ratepayers.

At our AGM in June 1986 we were justifiably full of complaints. After its final demise, the GLC had left in its coffers many millions of pounds which were available for handing back to those (like us) from whom it had originally been taken. City ratepayers should have received some £11.5 million recompense. In October we were allocated a derisory £71,000. The money had been taken from us on a rateable value basis and should have been returned on the same basis, the government agreeing that this was the right way but pressurised by the boroughs into distribution on a basis of population.

We protested on this and other rates issues via Peter Brooke. Our letter is published in full overleaf.

The response, from Dr Rhodes Boyson, was not particularly satisfactory, his line being that the government could not be seen to favour the City at the expense of the boroughs – which was of course the reverse of what had happened.

There was another problem – the government's proposal to replace domestic rates with a new 'Community Charge' based not on property values but the number of adults in a household. In itself, the new system was one of the best ideas to come from the Thatcher administration but again because of our tiny population, it would have led to rates bills for City residents of up to £14,000 a year! Happily, representations from Guildhall as well as from us led the government to make special arrangements for the City. Alas, this community charge (or 'poll tax' as it became pejoratively known) was the target for violent left-wing protest including a near-riot in Trafalgar Square. Eventually the government caved in. Domestic rates were finally scrapped as from April 1990 accompanied by abolition of the ILEA.

In September 1990 the Executive Committee decided that the Association had completed its work but rather than winding it up it should be 'placed in abeyance' for the time being – in case it became necessary to resume operations in the future. There was a brief resumption of activity in 1992 when, faced with changes from Community Charge to the new Council Tax, we foresaw a hefty increase in the amount City residents would be called upon to pay. Letters to all residents inviting them to join (or rejoin) the Association were delivered in June. In response to our invitation more than 400 residents signed up. We began our lobbying once again – with letters going to the Corporation and the government pointing out the substantial increases for City residents in the new Council Tax compared with the Community Charge – up from £360 for two people to as much as £780. In the light of our protests, the levels of Council Tax turned out to be a fair bit lower than forecast earlier.

As the new system became established there seemed to be no further action called for on our part. The Association was officially wound up in 2004.

A postscript to all this is that the creation by the government of a London Mayor and a 'Greater London Authority' is seeing the return of some of the disturbing features of the bad old days of the GLC. Although Mr Livingstone's current financial demands are still far from causing a public outcry, it is with a certain sense of déjà vu that one reads of the ever-increasing number of employees in the new London government and the increasing precepts now being levied by the Mayor on London boroughs and the City. Who knows, one of these days another battle may be necessary.

CITY OF LONDON RATEPAYERS' ASSOCIATION

Hon. Sec. Mrs. Valerie T. Meixner, 1 Milton Court, Barbican E.C.2.

Peter Brooke Esq., MP,
House of Commons,
LONDON SW1

28 October 1986

Dear Peter,

May I seek your aid in four matters affecting City of
London Ratepayers.

1. As you know, we lost out badly, and in our view most
    unfairly, in the distribution of the GLC balances.

    In 1986-7 we also lost out badly in regard to the
    Extended London Rate Equalization Scheme and we
    calculate that the City contribution to the scheme
    is £56 million higher than it should have been.

    A paper written by the Town Clerk points out that
    following GLC abolition some London boroughs gained
    hugely with substantial rate reductions of up to
    29 per cent being recorded. He commented: 'Certainly
    the Government's undertaking that authorities would
    not gain or lose relative to each other was not
    honoured for City ratepayers.'

    <u>Can we please hope that the Secretary of State will
    make some amends in his attitude to City ratepayers
    when he fixes Equalization sums in 1987-1988?</u>

2. A particular unfair point about Equalization is that
    domestic ratepayers are not receiving relief for the
    <u>additional</u> sums now being provided by the City in
    the form of the Extended Contribution. <u>Can we please
    expect relief under this heading?</u>

3. The Government's proposal for a 'community change'
    to replace domestic rates, while satisfactory for
    most parts of the country, is entirely inappropriate
    for City ratepayers whose bills would soar to
    astronomic levels. <u>Can we please be assured that the
    Government will make special arrangements for the
    City?</u>

4. The Government's proposals to collect business rates
    centrally and redistribute the money according to
    population would have the effect of increasing our
    business ratepayers' bills by some 30 per cent. <u>Can
    we please be assured that the Government will make
    special arrangements for the City?</u>

    This Association is non-party political but I should
    point out that the Government is getting bad
    publicity here on two counts:

(i) That the post GLC position has been unfair to City
    ratepayers and that the Government whom most, if not
    all, of our members have strongly supported in
    abolishing the GLC is seen to have treated us badly.

(ii)That the Government's sensible proposals for
    reforming the rates system are seen as posing a
    threat to both residential and business ratepayers
    and that to date there has been no single word of
    reassurance to us from the Government on these
    counts.

    The Committee of this Association – and indeed a far
    wider audience – would indeed be grateful if you
    could persuade the Secretary of State to treat the
    Government's friends with a little more
    consideration than has been the case in recent
    months!

Yours sincerely,

C. Douglas Woodward
Chairman

16

THE FIGHT TO SAVE MAPPIN & WEBB

The Queen was there in July 1982 to celebrate the opening, at long last, of the Barbican Centre when an impressive programme of music and theatre was attended by all the members of Common Council plus wives – except for me who was down with flu, Ann being accompanied that night by Lord Dowding, a Barbican neighbour. It was a good thing I was at home as one of the fireworks from St Giles' Terrace started a fire on our balcony which required extinguishing!

The Centre would become a central feature not only for our entertainment but also of internal strife within the Corporation as the years went by, but more of that later.

We had another long-awaited opening that year, of the new Billingsgate Market in Docklands just north of Canary Wharf.

For me, though, the major issue in 1982 was the beginning of the 'Mansion House Square' saga, with an application to redevelop the central area of the City around Mansion House with the creation of a new square in the centre of which would be an eighteen-storey tower block designed twenty years earlier by the modernist architect Mies van der Rohe (who had died in the interim). This scheme was the brainchild of Peter Palumbo who, with his father, had acquired over the years the twenty buildings contained within the triangle bounded by Poultry, Queen Victoria Street and Bucklersbury. At the apex of the triangle were jewellers Mappin & Webb. The Palumbo project would involved the destruction of Mappin & Webb and all the other notable Victorian buildings on this large site.

For the City Heritage Society I wrote to the City Architect:

> Given the existing street pattern at Bank junction it is inappropriate to superimpose a square [...] The destruction of buildings on the scale envisaged is not acceptable [...] The group of buildings in the triangle should be permanently rehabilitated because of their exceptional townscape value as well as their architectural quality [...] Especially important because of its key position is the Mappin & Webb building whose turret is such an outstandingly important feature [...] The tower block in this setting would be destructive of the character of the Bank conservation area [...] We regret the existing buildings have been allowed to deteriorate [...] the owners should be encouraged to carry out speedily a full-scale rehabilitation.

That was in February. By September the Planning Committee recommended rejection of the scheme, and when their report came to Common Council some unusually impassioned speeches from two or three of us persuaded everyone present that day in Guildhall to raise their hands in support.

It surely was a great victory for conservation and one in which elected members, Aldermen and Commoners were unanimously on the side of the angels. This attitude was in itself notable since, as I have already indicated, members of the Court were normally far from being conservation-minded. But Poultry and Mappin & Webb were special and close to members' hearts.

The story was, though, only beginning in September 1982. It would continue as a major theme running through the City's activities for more than a decade – and one in which the City Corporation could proudly declare that through all the forthcoming ups and downs it never once deviated from total opposition to Peter Palumbo's various schemes.

Needless to say he had not accepted our over-whelming rejection and appealed against it to the Secretary of State. A public enquiry took place between May and July 1984. Tom Wilmot, a fellow Councilman, and I gave evidence in support of the Corporation.

Later, Marcus Binney, chairman of Save Britain's Heritage, joined architect Terry Farrell in presenting their ideas for an excellent refurbishment of the Victorian buildings. Prince Charles in a famous speech likened the Palumbo tower to a 'glass stump' alongside the 'carbuncle on the face of a much-loved friend' as how he saw a proposal for an extension to the National Gallery.

A year later there was good news when Secretary of State Patrick Jenkin upheld his inspector's rejection of the Mansion House Square scheme – but, alas, he left the door open for an alternative 'new building of quality' when, of course, he should have called for a scheme of conservation.

Mr Palumbo was only too pleased to comply and had already commissioned another architect, James Stirling, to produce a different example of modern architecture. Mr Palumbo invited me over to his neo-Georgian office behind the church of St Stephen Walbrook (which he has generously endowed) where I was warmly welcomed by him and his rather splendid German shepherd. He said he would consult City Heritage when Stirling's scheme was ready. Although it was impossible for us to become friends I found him an agreeable man – just a pity that he had this obsession about having a modern building on this Victorian site which cried out to be preserved.

In fact, Stirling came up with two schemes, both retaining the triangular shape of the site, but the first one involved the demolition of all twenty existing buildings and replacing them with a single triangular wedge of seven storeys – likened by City Architect Stuart Murphy to a wedge of cheese and later by the Prince of Wales as looking like a 1930s wireless set. The second scheme retained the Mappin & Webb facade at least but would destroy everything else and would include a 150-foot-high tower, totally ruining the east-west view from the Royal Exchange along Cheapside to St Paul's. The medieval lane of Bucklersbury would disappear in both schemes.

Both schemes were considered quite wrong. That was in 1986.

A year later Palumbo had settled on the first of the

Stirling schemes – the wedge of cheese – and in June 1987 the Planning Committee, by a narrow majority, rejected it. When their report came to full Common Council there was again an overwhelming vote against.

Another year and in 1988 another public enquiry. City Heritage joined the Corporation and the national amenity societies in condemning Mr Palumbo's proposal, my City Heritage colleague Anthony Hemy and I giving evidence before the inspector. We argued that there was an extremely good refurbishment plan available, this one drawn up by English Heritage.

In July 1989, a new Secretary of State, Nicholas Ridley – most disastrous of environment ministers until John Prescott came on the scene many years later – went against his own inspector's decision and allowed Mr Palumbo's appeal. Disbelief and dismay all round, in the City, of course, but far beyond as well.

We in the Court of Common Council wished to apply for a judicial review but having taken counsel's opinion were advised that we should not spend rate-payers' money on further legal action. The fight would be continued by Save Britain's Heritage, led by Marcus Binney, who went for judicial review with City Heritage Society raising over £500 as a contribution to SAVE's (Save Britain's Heritage) substantial legal costs.

Alas, in early 1990 the judge in the High Court ruled there were no grounds in law to upset the Secretary of State's decision. SAVE immediately appealed, raising money in all manner of ways including getting a host of artists to produce paintings of Mappin & Webb which went on sale one evening at the galleries on the Mall. We have a splendid watercolour of that famous building hanging in our Barbican flat, a constant reminder of an outstanding City landmark that should never, ever, have been lost.

In March that year the City was celebrating a most famous victory when the Court of Appeal quashed the High Court ruling, Lord Justice Woolf saying that the Ridley decision was 'fatally flawed' in that he had failed to give adequate reasons for his departure from established government policy on listed buildings.

By then we had a much better Secretary of State in John Patten and as Chairman of City Heritage I wrote to him immediately urging him not to appeal to the House of Lords but to encourage refurbishment of the Poultry buildings. Commendably under their new master the Department of the Environment decided to let matters rest – but Mr Palumbo, not unexpectedly, submitted his own appeal. The final outcome remained in the balance.

Jenny Page, then chief executive of English Heritage, gave that year's City Heritage Lecture and was cheered to the rafters by the City audience that evening when she said: 'The No. 1 Poultry application was not only for the demolition of eight listed buildings but threatened the whole of the Bank conservation area. There is a constant temptation for owners to seek overdevelopment in areas already crowded.'

Just twelve months after the euphoria over the famous victory in the Court of Appeal came gloom and despondency with the House of Lords judges deciding in favour of Lord Palumbo as he had then become. The death knell was sounded for the end of the most famous of all planning battles in the City.

The Times, in a notable leading article, said of the proposed development that it was 'sheer destruction, a monumental act of egotism', a verdict with which a great many of us in the City would never come to disagree.

There are a couple of postscripts to the Poultry story. In 1993, following yet another public enquiry at which we had objected to the 'stopping up' of Bucklersbury (the medieval lane which would be lost in the Palumbo scheme), the Secretary of State (for Transport this time) dismissed his own inspector's recommendations thus giving the all-clear for Lord Palumbo's project.

It was ironic that it should fall to me as Chief Commoner at that time to have to announce in Common Council that this final obstacle to the development had been removed – a statement greeted with sympathetic laughter by the members.

Just after the Stirling building was completed I met Lord Palumbo in Walbrook. He asked me if, now it was finished, I liked it. I told him that I hated it – and still today it is a building I am happy to avoid.

Mappin & Webb, an outstanding City building which the Corporation fought so hard to save.
Picture courtesy of Guildhall Library

17

A GAGGLE OF TOWN CLERKS…
AND WE HAVE A LADY LORD
MAYOR

During my years on the Court, the City Corporation was served by five Town Clerks, each one excellent in his own way and justifiably proud of the standing of their historic office, one of the most sought-after appointments in local government – and not just because of the salary! Regrettably, the Corporation has now decided to go half-way with the tide and call its highest official Town Clerk and Chief Executive.

My first Town Clerk was Sir Edward Nichols, unusual in that he had been awarded a knighthood. It is the Town Clerk who conducts the meetings of Common Council and (with a little help from his two senior assistants) is expected to know by name every one of the Councilmen who rises to speak in Great Hall. I was much relieved when, as a new boy, Sir Edward recognised me on my first attempt.

Nichols retired in 1974 having served the Corporation for twenty years. He was succeeded by Stanley Clayton who did such an excellent job over the next eight years, to be followed in turn by Geoffrey Rowley who was, I think, one of the members' favourites. The high officers at Guildhall are elected by the whole Court of Common Council. For the two who have got through all the earlier stages of selection it must be something of an ordeal to stand on the dais in front of the Lord Mayor and facing a sea of some 150 faces, to know that success will depend on your short speech and the way you impress this critical audience. I was delighted when the vote was overwhelmingly in Geoffrey's favour and to congratulate him outside in the ambulatory, where he was clearly moved by his success.

In 1991, we elected Sam Jones – this time on the basis of a five-year contract – and he was to be the Town Clerk with whom I would have close dealings as Chief Commoner shortly afterwards. Sam came in with a misguided brief to reduce the large number of Corporation committees and departments but he was quickly made aware that committees and departments were having none of it. A later incumbent was more successful in this but in those days members were much more determined to maintain the status quo, I certainly being among them.

Sam settled down to be an outstandingly good Town Clerk. Alas, his five-year contract was not renewed in 1996 when the powers-that-be desired that Bernard Harty, the Chamberlain, should double up as Town Clerk. It seemed to me a job that would demand too much of one man and I got up and said so in Common Council, much as I liked him. In fact, his three-year term in this double job was highly successful, and he was always one of the most effective and accessible of officers.

City Under Attack Yet Again

In 1983 the GLC, its own days numbered, was still looking for targets to attack and one it all too readily lighted upon was the City of London Police which Paul Boateng, (later an MP and minister but then Chairman of the GLC Police Committee) said should be merged with the Met. Ivan Luckin, Chairman of our Police Committee vowed to fight this silly, possibly spiteful idea – and he had plenty of ammunition.

On one occasion I recall talking to HM Chief Inspector of Constabulary at the Home Office who, when he found I was to do with the City, told me that at every one of their regular inspections the City Police invariably scored top marks. How lucky we are in the City to have this small force serving a small area and doing it so effectively. There must be a lesson in this!

Much of the credit for this success rests with a succession of excellent Commissioners, as we call our police chiefs in the City. My favourite was Jim Page, a real copper's copper, burly, genial, loving the City, its pageantry – and dinners – and very good at his job. Ann and I and Jim and his wife Shirley (before she married another Woodward – though no relation) became good friends, exchanging dinners at our flat in the Barbican and their flat at the top of Wood Street Police Station.

Alas, in 1976, Jim left the City to become one of HM Inspectors of Constabulary for the north-west region and he died quite unexpectedly a short time afterwards.

About this time Gwyneth Dunwoody MP who would later become one of Labour's most sensible of backbenchers, but then Chairman of the party's regional and local government committee, gave voice to Labour's old song that 'in the interests of democracy' as soon as the party regained power it would abolish the City Corporation – and for good measure they would get rid of the shire counties at the same time!

The answer to that bit of nonsense, as far as the City was concerned, came via an opinion poll conducted by the *City Recorder* newspaper which found that among City residents 94% wanted to keep the City just as it was. We preferred our kind of democracy to anything her party could provide!

Goodbye Salvage Corps

In 1983 the City lost one of its institutions when the London Salvage Corps, with its station on the corner of Aldersgate Street and Long Lane, was closed down by the insurance companies, together with the two similar corps in Glasgow and Liverpool. For nearly 100 years the Salvage Corps vehicles had accompanied fire brigade engines to fires in commercial buildings, particularly in the docks, to salvage what they could of goods from the effects of fire, smoke and water. With the demise of the docks in these three cities there seemed little work left for the salvage men and salvage became another task for the fire brigades themselves. It's an ill wind…and the Aldersgate premises would provide an excellent new headquarters for my own Fire Protection Association!

With plenty to do for the FPA (on behalf of the insurance industry our job was to try to reduce fire losses) I had not been over-anxious to go for committee chairmanships at Guildhall but, in 1983, I became Deputy Chairman of our Libraries, Art Galleries and Records Committee, and began a long and highly enjoyable involvement with this most interesting of all Guildhall activities. More of that later.

First Lady Lord Mayor

On a rather higher level was the election that year of Alderman Mary Donaldson as our first (and to date) only lady Lord Mayor. Margaret Thatcher, her chief guest at the November banquet in Guildhall, still enormously popular, told us in her speech that her first concern was to address the increase in crime and hooliganism by the young – unlike more recent utterances by politicians we felt she really meant it, too!

Hooliganism was rearing its ugly head – and in some unexpected quarters. In April 1984 an unholy alliance of animal rights and anti-war demonstrators staged their first 'Stop the City' campaign and, although they certainly failed to stop the City, they did £100,000 worth of damage, smashing shop and bank windows, with Fenchurch Street and Lombard Street particular targets for their vandalism. 'Vile creatures' was how I described them in a Guildhall debate soon afterwards. By the time they tried again in October the City police were more ready for them and, with City workers vociferous in their condemnation damage was minimal.

With our first (and so far only) lady Lord Mayor,
Mary Donaldson, at a City Heritage Award in Cornhill;
the Master Painter-Stainer is on the right

There was much talk in those days about police officers being Freemasons, and the Commissioner of the City Police felt it necessary to say that this was not the case with him and his senior colleagues.

Sir Anthony Joliffe, Lord Mayor a year before, had something to say about the coal miners' strike: 'Scargill's strike is not about coal or miners but about destroying democracy'. Oddly enough, although Arthur Scargill had a flat in one of the Barbican tower blocks, I never once saw him in those tempestuous times. Not much of a loss perhaps.

On a happier note Princess Anne became Master of

the Farriers livery company in September 1984. At the Barbican Centre they had their first major conference event when over 3,000 delegates worldwide came to the City for the International Congress of Pharmacology.

Never a dull moment in the City!

18

UPS AND DOWNS IN CRIPPLEGATE AND HOW 'BIG BANG' WOULD CHANGE THE FACE OF CITY ARCHITECTURE

Cripplegate celebrated in 1985 the election as Lord Mayor of its own Alderman, Allan Davis, the beginning of an outstanding mayoralty in which we Cripplegate Councilmen would share. What I specially remember were Allan's speeches. Of course all Lord Mayors have a speechwriter – with the hundreds of speeches they are called on to make they clearly need assistance, but it soon became clear that this Lord Mayor was injecting his own thoughts into these events, making each of them special to the occasion and his audience. Not every Lord Mayor takes quite so much trouble.

At the Lord Mayor's Banquet in November there was a standing ovation for Norman Tebbit and his wife Margaret, paralysed in the IRA bomb attack at Brighton, when he pushed her wheelchair down the aisle to be greeted by the new Lord Mayor.

Less happy for Cripplegate as it was to turn out was the election of one Derek Palmer at our Ward election in December 1985 – a nice enough man, but with an overriding ambition to be top of the annual poll. From then on the atmosphere among the Cripplegate members would change.

Hitherto the members standing for re-election each December, eleven or twelve of us, would present ourselves in a joint election address, each of us telling the voters what they had done during the past year and their priorities for the future. We would share the printing costs and each would undertake a share of the deliveries into letterboxes. This system was not only convenient for the members but we believed that residents and business voters preferred to have one piece of paper delivered to them rather than eleven or twelve separate ones – plus of course any from people newly offering themselves for election. Behind this practice was a long-established camaraderie – we were competing, but as friends. After all, the annual Ward elections to Common Council were not exactly earth-shattering events and it was generally felt that we could be relaxed about them.

Derek Palmer, however, thought otherwise, and in December 1986 he said he would be standing alone. Others feared they would be at a disadvantage and said they too would issue their own election address. Seven of us stayed together that year. A welcome addition to our number was Stella Currie, recent Chairman of the Barbican Association with whom I had worked closely on such matters as City rates.

In December 1987, Barbara Keep stood for election under Palmer's protective wing. He topped the poll with 221 votes having pulled out all the stops. Barbara was second with 215. Joined with the old hands I was third with 208. However much one strove there was not all that much difference in the election results!

The tragedy that night was that one of the three contenders not elected – fifteen had stood – was Wilfrid Dewhirst, Ward Deputy and the man who back in 1971 had pioneered the entry of Barbican residents on to Common Council. His 'crime' was that he was no longer living in the Barbican. For him it was a truly devastating election night. Allan Davis, the presiding Alderman, appointed me as Deputy in his place but my concern for Wilfrid clouded the pleasure I would otherwise have felt. Derek Balls, the only other non-resident, remained as fellow Ward Deputy – but his low vote must have told him how the wind was blowing in Cripplegate.

Wilfrid Dewhirst's defeat signalled the beginning of a campaign by Derek Parker and others not only to get rid of anyone not resident in Barbican but anyone else who, for some reason or another, they did not like.

Barbara Keep and her husband Derek were good friends of Ann and myself and she would become one of the most popular of the Cripplegate Councilmen, very active in the Ward and with much to her credit. But as time went on I found myself increasingly irked by the way she positively encouraged people to stand at the annual elections with a view to knocking someone else off. Sometimes the favourites themselves fell into disfavour and realised their days on the Court were numbered. At least I remained her friend although as Deputy I had on occasion to take her to task!

'Big Bang'

For the City – and far wider afield – the most important event of this time was the deregulation in

1986 of the London Stock Exchange – 'Big Bang' as the newspapers were to call it, turning the City's traditional financial workings on their head. The 'City man' with bowler hat and pinstripe suit would give way to youthful dealers speaking estuary English. The repercussions were enormous, not least for property development, and thus for City Heritage.

The trade journal *Building* had this to say:

> The City Corporation set off a developers' free-for-all at London Wall. What makes London Wall suddenly so ripe for development is its disastrous 1960s architecture with tower blocks that cannot cope with the demands of the electronic office of the 1980s, never mind the large floorplate financial dealing floors needed for Big Bang. The City Corporation is falling over itself to cater for the Big Bang's supposedly gargantuan appetite for offices.

A wind of change was certainly blowing hard through the City, led by a new star in the property firmament, Councilman and City solicitor Michael Cassidy, an old friend whose rapid rise in Common Council led to his election in 1986 as Chairman of the Planning Committee.

His positive leanings towards big office developments would soon cut across the more conservationist approach of City Architect Stuart Murphy, who would shortly resign to be replaced by his deputy Peter Rees – himself with a background in conservation but far more willing to 'move with the times', as it were, and to work with Cassidy in pursuing a new Corporation vision for the City's office development. With Stuart Murphy's departure the office of City Architect was lost and Peter Rees became our first City Planning Officer.

The City of London 'Local Plan', substantially modified in response to pressure from the powerful property lobby, was opening the way for massive new buildings, the first of them being a replacement for Lee House, one of those 1960s 'shoebox' towers, on the corner of London Wall and Wood Street. The replacement, designed by architect Terry Farrell, would span London Wall and be three times the size of Lee House. The Planning Committee approved it.

In those days Common Council had the final say over such planning decisions and when it came before us, speeches by Alderman Tony Bull, an independent spirit though in the property world himself, and I managed to persuade the Court to reject it by fifty-seven votes to fifty-six. Bull and I had a meeting with Farrell and he agreed to reduce his mammoth slightly – not nearly enough in our view but when it came back to Common Council we knew that further objection would be useless. This was the start for the succession of skyscrapers and groundscrapers which would, over the years, quite change the City's architectural character.

19

TROUBLES OVER CANARY WHARF AND THE DELIGHTS OF CHAIRING THE LIBRARY COMMITTEE

Early days still for Canary Wharf in 1986 but some in the Corporation felt a tremor of concern at possible future competition. Such a pity that the City had not bought in to the still inexpensive property opportunities there and thus lay claim to, say, 51% of Canary Wharf development potential, making it the ideal City overspill for the tower blocks to come. Robin Leigh-Pemberton, that splendid governor of the Bank of England, said he saw the need for an extension of the City to the Wharf to ensure the future supply of office space.

The Corporation's unease was first evidenced in its attitude to the Docklands Light Railway, then under construction, which the developer wanted to terminate right in the City's centre at Bank underground station. The Corporation argued that it should finish at Cannon Street.

There were, indeed, solid grounds for opposing a Bank terminus since adding yet another line would make existing congestion even worse. Peter Rigby, Policy Committee Chairman, went so far as to offer the DLR a million pounds to finance the Cannon Street option. The Corporation then petitioned the government to agree this course which Michael Heseltine, the Environment Secretary, described as the City's attempt to 'scupper' Canary Wharf, and the petition was roundly rejected by the House of Commons in June 1986.

It never seemed to me that the City was really bent on scuppering Canary Wharf, and I said as much to Docklands people when we had a City Heritage visit there in the summer, but I was aware that my assurances were viewed somewhat sceptically in that quarter.

Later, when the link to Bank was actually under construction, a more immediate problem was that the tunnelling work seriously undermined the structural integrity of the Mansion House, necessitating massive underpinning of the eighteenth century Grade I-listed building.

Later still when Alderman Peter Levene found himself under attack for having become Canary Wharf chairman, I said in Common Council that we should really stop worrying about competition from that quarter since the City had all the trump cards in attracting companies to operate in the Square Mile rather than on the Isle of Dogs. I suppose that recent moves by the HSBC bank and solicitors Clifford Chance from the City to Canary Wharf may suggest otherwise but I still feel that most of the advantages lie with the City.

Indeed, now that all the surrounding boroughs are striving to have office towers of their own perhaps it does not really matter. The great thing is for the City to keep its own distinctive character as the natural centre for doing international business, and in my view that does not require any more office towers!

Queen Mother Becomes a Bummaree

What else was happening in the City in 1986?

The butchers at Smithfield – and all the rest of us, especially the newspapers – were delighted when the Queen Mother was made a bummaree, thus earning the right to a meat porter's licence in the market.

With the Queen Mother at the Mansion House where she enjoyed seeing the Samuel collection of Dutch paintings

Margaret Thatcher inaugurated the great Broadgate development behind Liverpool Street Station – and Stuart Lipton provided us all with a celebration lunch.

I cannot think why in City Heritage we never gave him an award for what was a very civilised piece of City development. We did give Quinlan Terry the City Heritage Award that year for his outstanding refurbishment of the 'Bengal' warehouse at Cutlers Gardens. It was a pity that Quinlan Terry was not invited to do more work in the City – his style and flair could have produced some splendid, traditional, architecture that we would all have been proud of. He certainly could have done wonders for Paternoster! We did have the sense to throw out an absurd scheme for a thirty-one-storey tower replacement for Winchester House along London Wall.

The Labour Party set up a branch in the Barbican saying it would put up people to fight ward elections in the City and 'get rid of the class-oriented Lord Mayor'. In December 1986, for the first time in thirty years, we thus had party political candidates standing for election in the three City wards with large residential populations – Aldersgate, Cripplegate and Portsoken. In all three they failed dismally at the polls.

Chairman of the Library Committee

I enjoyed a double helping of glory at the beginning of the year having been declared Deputy Governor of the Honourable the Irish Society, the oldest of all the Common Council committees and one which takes precedence, and soon afterwards being elected Chairman of the City's Libraries, Art Galleries and Records Committee.

I had already been Deputy Chairman of Libraries

for three years, rather longer than was customary, but Chairman David Shalit (a good friend) liked the job so much that he stayed on for an extra year over and above the three it was customary to serve. His reason was that with the winding up of the GLC, the City had taken over responsibility for running the Greater London Records Office, and he felt it would be sensible for the existing chairman to see this important change through. Later, after I had done my three year stint as Chairman, I found an equally satisfactory reason to ask the committee for a fourth year!

The Libraries Committee was my long-time favourite and I was a member for no less than seventeen years in all. Other Cripplegate members who could have asked for a turn were most forbearing and left me to enjoy myself.

It was a committee full of interest and variety – we looked after the Guildhall Library, three lending libraries, and the printing library at St Bride's; the Guildhall Art Gallery collection and the Barbican Art Gallery; the City Records Office and the newly acquired Greater London Records Office. So much richness. It was also a committee where members felt they could make a real input, effect changes and get things done.

The Guildhall Library was, I suppose, the jewel in the crown. Founded in 1420, the modern institution dates from 1824, and when I first came into the City, back in 1964, it was still housed in a splendid Victorian building attached to Guildhall. Mr Librarian occupied a rather grand chandelier-lit chamber adjoining. Now the Guildhall Library is part of the new West Wing of

Guildhall, its original premises are called the Old Library and are used for receptions and dinners. Mr Librarian's room became the Chief Commoner's Parlour.

The Library is a treasure-house of London life past and present, books, periodicals and such special collections as those devoted to Samuel Pepys and John Wilkes. The renowned Print Room has London maps from the sixteenth century onwards. The manuscripts section has holdings from the eleventh century including the records of Christ's Hospital and Trinity House. (Records of the first thirty years of the City Heritage Society are now lodged there too.)

The Corporation's rich collection of art was, in my day, largely stored in the cellars beneath Guildhall, with pictures being loaned for display to the Mansion House, Central Criminal Court and a few other special places. Now the collection is housed in the handsome new Guildhall Art Gallery.

But in my years as Chairman of the Committee we did have another art gallery in our keeping – that within the Barbican Arts Centre. It was a quite deliberate decision, when the Barbican Centre was being created, that it should contain a lending library and an art gallery, both of which would be the responsibility of the Library Committee. However, not long after the Centre opened there grew a feeling within the new Barbican Centre Committee that the art gallery should come to them – a view certainly promoted by successive directors of the Centre. David Shalit, and then I, were able for years to withstand the periodic attempts to pluck the gallery from our grasp, arguing that it was clearly beneficial to have two strong committees involved in the Centre's affairs (and two separate sources of funding) and that in any event we were the Corporation's experts on pictures! It was some years later that the Centre finally got its way.

There were numerous royal visitors to the Centre and its first director, Henry Wrong, would greet them on their arrival at the Silk Street entrance and conduct them to whatever it was they were attending. This he did also when the royal was coming to the art gallery, which led to problems.

It was, I think, Prince Michael of Kent who had accepted an invitation to open our great exhibition of Russian art treasures. The Lord Mayor, Lady Mayoress, Ann and I were waiting with the curator to welcome him to the gallery and then to show him around. Henry Wrong decreed that security demanded he alone could do this, the rest of us ordered to remain well to the rear. The Lord Mayor was not amused (nor was I) and had Henry at the Mansion House next day to express this displeasure. At least we were spared any reoccurrence of that bit of officiousness.

Other royal visitors were welcomed and shown around rather less formally. The Duchess of York (in the briefest of leather miniskirts) said to Ann: 'Behind every successful man is an exhausted woman' when she opened one of our shows. Prince Edward, who did the honours for our Edwardiana exhibition told us in the lift going up to the Gallery that he did enjoy life but the Palace tended to leave him somewhat in the dark about his engagements.

*With Princess Anne at a Library Committee reception;
Melvyn Barnes, Libraries Director, is talking to the Princess*

One evening, when we had two exhibition openings, I did one myself and we had Sir Edward Heath to open the other. Afterwards, as was our invariable custom, we invited him to have a celebratory drink in our private enclosure. That was just after seven o'clock. 'Well,' he said, 'just one, as my driver is waiting below to take me back to Salisbury.' At nine, Ann and I (hungry) wished him goodnight and left him surrounded by an admiring throng while he continued talking – very knowledgeably – about painting and his own fine collection.

Ann and I welcome Prince Edward and Lord Mayor Robin Gillett to the Barbican Art Gallery where the prince would open the 'Edwardian Era' exhibition

We did put on some really splendid shows in the gallery – the pictures of David Roberts, Gwen John, James Tissot, and Lowry come specially to mind, all of them very well attended.

In 1987, the notable collection of Dutch paintings built up by Sir Harold Samuel was, on his death, bequeathed to the City – with the explicit condition that it should be hung in its entirety in the Mansion House, in the Lord Mayor's keeping, as it were. This gift had been arranged by Sir Robert Bellinger, a friend of the Samuel family and Lord Mayor himself in 1966. This splendid bequest brought with it a great deal of trouble – particularly for the Chairman of the Library Committee and for our art collection curator Vivien Knight.

C. Douglas Woodward
Chairman of the Libraries,
Art Galleries and Records Committee,
Corporation of the City of London
cordially invites you to a Private View
of the exhibition

The Image of London
Views by Travellers and Emigrés
1550-1920

on Wednesday 5 August 1987: 6–8pm
at Barbican Art Gallery
(Level 8) Barbican Centre
London EC2Y 8DS

Another of our Barbican exhibitions, 'The Image of London',
with Tissot decorating the invitation card

Not long after I had announced the acquisition in Common Council and the pictures had been painstakingly hung on the first floor of the Mansion House came the first cries of distress from the then

Lord Mayor and Lady Mayoress who were bitterly upset to have had their lovely Tissots taken from the walls and replaced with eighty rather small paintings, the details of which were hard to make out.

Lighting this unique collection was the biggest problem and the complaints went on through at least three mayoralties and numerous summonses for me and Vivien to attend the Mansion House, until eventually, with a completely new lighting system using fibre optics, a degree of contentment was achieved. I did sometimes wonder whether it was a gift we could have done without. Then, one afternoon, Ann and I were present in Mansion House and the Queen Mother, who had been having tea in the Egyptian Hall, forsook the teacups for champagne in the Drawing Room to admire the Samuel pictures. She told us that she thought they were lovely and that day it all seemed very worthwhile.

20

THE HONOURABLE THE IRISH SOCIETY

My association with Northern Ireland had begun in the early 1980s with visits to Belfast for meetings of the Northern Ireland Fire Liaison Panel – one of a string of such panels we had set up across the UK to combat escalating fire losses – none more necessary, one might have thought, than in Northern Ireland although, terrorism apart, the people there were rather better than most in avoiding accidental fires!

Another dimension opened with membership of the Honourable the Irish Society and my appointment in January 1986 as its Deputy Governor, the beginning of one of the most enjoyable experiences of my years on Common Council and one which Ann and I would share.

The Honourable the Irish Society is as steeped in the City's history as are the mayoralty and shrievalty. It is the oldest of all of the Corporation's committees, enjoying a degree of precedence over all the rest, having come into being during the troubles in Ireland, particularly in the rebellious north, during the reigns of Elizabeth I and then James I who, with his ministers, saw, as a solution to constant uprisings against English rule, the establishment there of a Protestant colony of English and Scots settlers. This Ulster 'plantation' would inevitably be a costly enterprise and, as has so frequently happened over the centuries, the king looked to the City of London for money. The City Corporation, supported by the City's fifty-five livery companies were invited – perhaps 'instructed' is the better word – to take over and run a large part of the plantation, an area that would become the county of Londonderry centred around Derry and Coleraine.

It was argued by the king that this new possession – like Virginia or the East India Company – would be a profitable undertaking for the City's merchants and traders and would offer the additional benefit of ridding the overcrowded City of some of its surplus population! The Corporation – and the livery companies who were to provide the money – were understandably sceptical seeing little benefit and less profit coming to them from these distant and troubled estates. They were in fact dragged reluctantly into the enterprise on royal insistence. It was thus that the Honourable the Irish Society was established under Royal Charter.

Over the next years it proved increasingly difficult for the Corporation to raise the amount of money demanded by the Crown, the situation worsening with the accession of Charles I. Amid increasing acrimony between king and corporation, the Star Chamber pronounced the Charter of the Irish Society to have been abrogated, the king taking over the Society's possessions for his own use. In 1641, at a banquet in

Guildhall arranged as a peace-offering, King Charles promised that the Star Chamber's judgement would be reversed. However, war in Ireland and then civil war in England prevented that promise from being fulfilled. The Irish question was undoubtedly one of the reasons for the City backing Parliament and Cromwell against the king.

It was not until Charles II was restored to the throne that in 1662 the Irish Society was fully reinstated with a new Royal Charter giving it Londonderry (as Derry would henceforth be known) and Coleraine in perpetuity, together with all the surrounding lands and the rivers Bann and Foyle so rich in salmon and the eel fishing, said to be finest in Europe.

The plantation developed, its agricultural and fishing resources augmented to include the trades and crafts introduced by the livery companies. Apprentices, first from Christ's Hospital and then many more, were brought in. The walls of Londonderry, the last of Europe's fortified cities, were built and the cathedral of St Columb founded by the Irish Society.

The walls, such a splendid feature still there today, had their most famous moment in 1689 when their gates were shut by the apprentices to protect the Protestant inhabitants and garrison from a besieging army led in the Catholic cause by King James II, supported by the French king. The siege of Londonderry lasted 105 days and by the time it was over Londonderry had been devastated. There was much for the Irish Society to do in the following years to restore some prosperity to its property.

Even in its early days, the Society regarded itself as a trustee for the public good and that income from its holdings should go, as it did, on public works, provision of education and charitable giving. The livery companies who had provided the money originally believed that the Society's income was held in trust for them and, indeed, until 1830 the companies did receive their modest share.

From then on everything earned by the Society has been ploughed back to benefit the people of County Londonderry. Schools were built and maintained, support provided for hospitals, bridges and quays built, a water-supply system created, new churches endowed, Londonderry's Guildhall built and vast improvements made on the River Bann.

In more recent times the income from the Society's property holdings has been made available in grants to hundreds of worthy causes with an underlying objective of fostering good relations between the two communities. Once regarded with some suspicion the Society has come to be recognised as a power for good in the land.

It was therefore something of an honour to be appointed Deputy Governor of the Honourable the Irish Society, to follow in the footsteps of the many distinguished men who had held that office over three centuries. The Society has always been headed as Governor by an Alderman who had already served as Lord Mayor. Barrett Manning, then the long-serving Secretary to the Society, told me in 1986 that the Governor was akin to the chairman of a company, the Deputy Governor its managing director and that is certainly how it worked.

The Court of Common Council also appoints a Court of Assistants to help Governor and Deputy Governor in conducting the Society's business. Its meetings took place (in my day) in the handsome Irish Chamber (1824) in Guildhall Yard. Three times a year a small group of members went on 'visitations' to County Londonderry, staying at the Society's other house, Georgian of course, in the centre of Londonderry, under the city walls. My first visitation, in 1982, was at the height of the IRA troubles of which we were reminded by seeing armed soldiers regularly doing their 'sweeps' outside our windows. One was recommended not to walk the walls alone after dark.

The Governor normally leads the spring and summer visitations, the Deputy Governor that in October. The summer visit was the longest with the added attraction of having the Governor's and Deputy Governor's wives with us. Ann and I had a great time in June 1986 with Sir Peter and Lady Gadsden – Peter and Belinda being friends and neighbours in the Barbican.

A strong constitution was essential on these visits – not least a good digestion. A substantial breakfast to set you up for the morning visits and meetings, then lunch with a few guests before another series of visits including school prize-givings with the Governor and I taking it in turns to hand out the awards, these occasions invariably culminating in vast teatime spreads over which the staff had taken so much trouble that one had to tuck in. Back to the house for a brief rest before welcoming our guests for dinner – civic, church and business leaders and perhaps the officer commanding the local troops.

Presentation of £3,000 to the Foyle Hospice by Irish Society Governor, Peter Gadsden, and Deputy Governor (on right)

Grace was said before we sat down but these events differed from every other City dinner in that we did not toast the Queen at the end – to spare the feelings of any republican guests. Perhaps we were being over-cautious? Sunday morning saw us in our Cathedral of St Columb.

Part of each visitation took us to Coleraine where we stayed in a hotel and enjoyed the cooking at the Salmon Leap restaurant presided over in great style by the sister of the Irish prime minister, Miss Haughy. In Coleraine we were especially concerned with the River Bann and the sales and rental income from its salmon fishing. There were perennial problems with our elvers which were substantially poached by a cleric with IRA connections, the eels finishing up on Dutch rather than UK dinner plates.

Occasionally, in June, there was time to relax and on the 1986 visitation we had an afternoon off at the Giant's Causeway. On the way there we dropped in to pay our respects to the Bushmills distillery – only right and proper in view of our not inconsiderable intake of their splendid Black Bush label!

21

THE PRINCE OF WALES LAMBASTS THE ARCHITECTS AND WE ENTERTAIN KING FAHD

The year 1987 was, as ever, full of activity for the City. In January, Edwina Coven became our first lady Chief Commoner. Lord Mayor David Rowe-Ham, speaking at the United Wards Club banquet, attacked the 'bizarre tactics used in the Guinness takeover of the Distillers Company'. The Bishop of Durham, the ever-controversial David Jenkins, speaking in St Michael's Cornhill attacked the 'outrageous' salaries paid in the City – goodness knows what he would have said about the handouts in 2006–2007!

The London Residuary Body – doling out the bits of the GLC's former empire – said the City was on the shortlist to take over Hampstead Heath. In March, the Corporation, competing only with Camden Council, offered £1 million a year towards the cost of running the Heath provided the LRB would set up a trust fund of £15 million to yield the other £800,000 which was needed. The City would shortly get Hampstead Heath mainly in recognition of its excellent record with Epping Forest, Burnham Beeches and many other open spaces in London.

The Rape of Paternoster

On the architectural front there was another scheme for Paternoster Square. City Heritage expressed disappointment at the choice of architects – Richard Rogers, James Stirling, the Foster Practice – saying that we needed people with a greater feel for the traditional style of City buildings.

It was later that year that Prince Charles, speaking at the Planning Committee Dinner in Mansion House, spoke of the earlier 'rape of Paternoster Square', and roundly accused planners, architects and developers of wrecking the London skyline and desecrating the dome of St Paul's. He told his 200-strong audience that the City now had a second chance and should have as its vision a city without towers. 'Do we still have to strive to be a stunted version of Manhattan?' he asked. My admiration for the Prince of Wales, already of the highest, soared yet higher. It has been a lasting regret that just this once I was not present that night to applaud, having had to go to Hong Kong for one of my fire conferences.

On a somewhat different level, Farringdon Common Councilman Edward Clements proposed a motion in Common Council to ban the 'loving cup' ceremony, a rite hallowed by time which formed an essential conclusion to livery company dinners and many of those at the Mansion House. The reason for Clements' motion was growing concern about AIDS, although it is doubtful whether the rim of the loving cup could result in such dire consequences. About that time Noel Mander, builder of church organs, nudged me in the ribs when we were about to partake in the loving cup at Apothecaries Hall, and said *sotto voce* 'I wouldn't drink any of that if I were you'. Another diner was quoted in the *City Recorder* as saying the loving cup should certainly go because the contents (sack, a sherry-type wine) were 'sweet, sparkling and horrible'.

The ceremony has escaped unscathed to the present day, still a rather agreeable accompaniment to City dinners.

London City Airport Opens

In June 1987, the first Dash 7 propeller-driven aircraft took off on a trial basis from the new London City Airport, the airport opening for business in October, and transforming the ease of travel to Paris, Brussels and Zurich.

I was an early traveller, relishing the short taxi ride from the City, the almost total lack of other passengers and the five-minute passage through passport control via duty-free shops to the steps of the little aircraft. Aboard, the champagne was served immediately. Alas, on my first flight (to Paris), just as we cleared the City, I saw from my cabin window one of the two propellers slow down and stop. I wondered whether the pilot had noticed. He had, and after circling the towers of the Barbican a dozen times we finished up at Stanstead. All other journeys were perfect except for the fact that while London City Airport was so people-free and easy, one still arrived at ghastly Charles de Gaulle at the other end. But what a treat it was after Heathrow!

Our newest livery hall, jointly owned by the Farmers and Fletchers, was opened by Princess Anne in June. She was always a favourite with the livery companies and closely involved with those having riding associations, becoming Master of the Farriers Company. This year, too, she performed the opening ceremony of the City of London School, moved from the Victoria Embankment to Queen Victoria Street but still on the riverside. The school was the work of Stuart Murphy, the last building in the City to have the City Architect as its designer.

There was a general election in June 1987, with Mrs Thatcher back in office and Peter Brooke, our admirable member, was very comfortably returned. The Queen opened the Docklands Light Railway in August – its City terminal being at Bank Station. My friend Ian Rushton, head of the Royal Insurance Company, presented the Royal Shakespeare Company at the Barbican with a cheque for £1 million to rescue them from financial crisis. Royal Insurance – and even more so the City Corporation – were extraordinarily generous to the RSC, generosity that was ill-repaid, the company always complaining about the theatre we had provided for them and eventually pushing off – a relief to all although at the time their fairly abrupt departure was regarded as a loss.

Banquet for King Fahd

Two nice things happened to me in 1987. Attending the reception committee of thirty-three Aldermen and Councilmen appointed to manage the state visit of

King Fahd of Saudi Arabia, I put up for the chairman-ship and was elected. That was my first real taste of being in charge of organising one of these great City occasions, all enormously enjoyable.

Chairing the reception committee before the king's arrival

The banquet went off beautifully. One was presented to the king during the reception in the Old Library and, just before the dinner, we had champagne with him and the Duke and Duchess of Gloucester in the Print Room with other special guests.

Adrian Barnes, the Remembrancer[1], had assured me that

---

[1] Adrian Barnes had been appointed a year earlier and was the Remembrancer with whom I had most to do during my years on the court. Looking down from his 6 ft 4 in, he oversaw every one of our innumerable events with enormous ability and panache. In this he was maintaining an office established in 1570, the first holder, Sir Thomas Norton, being given the task 'to keep in remembrance' all dealings between City Corporation and the Queen.

all kinds of goodies would be forthcoming from the royal bounty afterwards, not least the gold watch presented almost as a matter of course by Arab potentates. In fact there had been some contretemps on the part of the king with the Palace and his generosity was tempered by disappointment – so no watches or medals. I must say that the whole event had been so very pleasurable that I really was looking for nothing more, although a pair of handsome gold cufflinks were delivered a day or so later, which I still occasionally wear.

The other nice thing that happened to me was that I was elected by Common Council as one of the Corporation's six Governors of the Museum of London, an office I would enjoy holding for the next ten years. Three others were Common Councilmen – Norman Harding, Michael Cassidy and Peter Revell-Smith. In addition, we had Dr Alan Clinton and Sir Ashley Bramall. Nine further governors were appointed by the prime minister, including Michael Robbins who was our Chairman. Max Hebditch was our esteemed Director.

We met every other month, and all of us greatly enjoyed playing our part in the running of this great museum. As I suppose with all our museums, money was a constant concern. Entry was free in those days (as it is again now) but I was one of those who argued the case for a modest entrance charge – not a popular view then although the Board of Governors reluctantly agreed to impose charges, not least to help with ambitious plans for renewal of galleries.

At the end of 1987, as I mentioned earlier, my good friend Wilfrid Dewhirst lost his place in Cripplegate and I was appointed Deputy for Cripplegate Within.

*The king conducted by the Lord Mayor into the
reception in the Old Library*

Corporation of London

RECEPTION and BANQUET

in honour of

The Custodian
of The Two Holy Mosques
King Fahd bin Abdulaziz Al-Saud
King of Saudi Arabia

GUILDHALL
Wednesday, 25th March, 1987

The Right Honourable the Lord Mayor
ALDERMAN SIR DAVID ROWE-HAM, GBE, DLitt

Sheriffs
MR. ALDERMAN HUGH BIDWELL
MR. ALDERMAN MICHAEL GRAHAM

Chairman of the Reception Committee
C. DOUGLAS WOODWARD, Esq

Menu card for our banquet in honour of King Fahd

MENU

Veuve Cliquot, N.V.

Mâcon Lugny 1985   Spitalfields Terrine

★ ★ ★

Baby Turbot with
Salmon Mousse
Fresh Lobster Sauce

★ ★ ★

Mango Sorbet

★ ★ ★

Château Pontet Clauzure 1982   Breast of Duckling
Grande Cru St. Emilion   with Pistachios and Apricots
Mange Tout
Stuffed Tomato with Spinach
and Nutmeg
Anna Style Potatoes

★ ★ ★

Laurent Perrier, N.V.   Riyadh Rondelle

★ ★ ★

Taylors LBV   Coffee
Hine VSOP   Petits Fours
Liqueurs

…and what we provided for the 700 to eat that night.

22

THE CITY ACQUIRES HAMPSTEAD HEATH

In 1988, the London Residuary Body awarded the running of Hampstead Heath to the City Corporation on the financial terms we had earlier stipulated, the takeover to become effective in April the following year.

The newest of our committees, the Hampstead Heath Management Committee, had twelve Common Councilmen on it, some appointed for one or two years, five of us for three years. Having lived in Hampstead for twenty years before moving into the Barbican, I was delighted to be in at the start of this new enterprise.

To underline our commitment that we would govern the Heath with full regard to local opinion, the Committee also included representatives from Camden and Barnet Councils, together with nominees from English Heritage (who ran the Kenwood part of the Heath), the Nature Conservancy Council and the Ramblers Association. We considered that the most important and formidable 'local' member was Peggy Jay, appointed by that notable amenity group, the Heath and Old Hampstead Society. Mrs Jay (wife of former Labour politician Douglas and mother of journalist, later ambassador, Peter) was herself a former Labour stalwart on the GLC, and from her we expected the most critical view of our doings.

To chair the committee we had the 'safest' pair of Corporation hands in Gordon Wixley and we were all enjoined to tread carefully in this new and possibly difficult terrain. To keep an eye on things the Deputy Town Clerk, no less, would sit in on each of our two-monthly meetings.

As it turned out, Peggy Jay became our greatest friend and ally. I liked to sit next to her at these meetings to enjoy her not so sotto voce asides. In 1996 she was delighted to be made a Freeman of the City. Another way of making sure that everyone living around the Heath felt their interests were being looked after was the setting up of a consultative group which met midway between our meetings, and comprised every conceivable local group. Sensibly this group met on the Heath in the superintendent's premises at Parliament Hill. Their views were fed into our deliberations and our proposals put first to them. From time to time members of the main committee set off from Guildhall in a small coach to tour sections of our domain, culminating with lunch in a splendid Italian café at Golders Hill Park.

During those years (I eventually became Deputy Chairman of the Committee) all went reasonably smoothly under the direction of Superintendent Paul Canneau. A concern was the increasing use of the Heath by 'cruising' homosexual men and the detritus left by them, particularly those on drugs. Some of our excellent Heath keepers became special constables, helping to control this unsavoury business.

Other than that, Peggy Jay and her Heath and Old Hampstead Society, and the local population in general, came to the conclusion that the Heath had never been better managed. Certainly the money we had available was put to good use in renewing paths, tree conservation and replanting, and provision of improved facilities for sports activities – running, football, swimming, tennis and bowls. It was all very worthwhile and my only regret was that retirement from the Common Council prevented my becoming Chairman of this most interesting committee.

City Awash with Office Space

There was a good deal going on in the planning world at the end of the 1980s. The *City Recorder* reported the Square Mile as being awash with empty office space – some three million square feet in 1988. A project to build a thirty-one-storey tower on London Wall was given short shrift by Common Council with Councilmen saying it would 'dominate the skyline half way between St Paul's and the NatWest Tower, diminishing the significant role of the cathedral'. Those were the days!

Prince Charles, in a television programme, likened the proposed scheme at No 1 Poultry to a 1930s wireless set and praised a new scheme for Paternoster by John Simpson, an architect who favoured a traditional style of building. Minster Court on Mincing Lane (I called it Monster Court in recognition of its 'Gothic' fins, angles and gables) was under way. The City Engineer told us that the 120-

year old Holborn Viaduct was cracking up and a £1 million programme to strengthen it was put in hand.

Plans to build a new art gallery in Guildhall Yard were thrown into disarray when remains of a Roman amphitheatre were discovered underneath. Coachloads of visitors arrived expecting, probably, to see rather more than the mere stone traces and outlines that were there but this 'priceless treasure' would receive full-scale protection, delaying the art gallery for years, but eventually becoming one of the City's great visitor attractions.

We were all delighted when, after a long campaign by Councilman Dr James Cope, a statue commemorating that famous reformer John Wilkes, the eighteenth-century Lord Mayor and Member of Parliament, was to be erected in Fetter Lane.

The summer of 1988 was particularly agreeable for me in that I was appointed OBE in the Queen's Birthday Honours. As was the custom on such occasions the honour was announced in Common Council by the Chief Commoner, Brian Wilson. The *City Recorder* published a nice picture of Ann and me at Buckingham Palace. Although the award was for 'services to fire safety' the *City Recorder* decided it was for being Chairman of the City Heritage Society, and Her Majesty had kind words for the City.

Our New Dean

We had a new Dean at St Paul's – the delightful Eric Evans, a conservative churchman in all senses of the word, in contrast to his predecessor Alan Webster. The

Dean was a welcome visitor to a great many City functions and got to know a good many Common Councilmen.

When I was Chief Commoner I was invited by him to a luncheon party in the Chapter House when one of the Cannons said, apropos of the Corporation, 'absolute Toy Town of course'. Toy Town had been a children's hour favourite on BBC radio featuring Mr Mayor, Larry the Lamb and Mr Grouser, and we identified their current counterparts in Common Council. The Cannon was doubtless thinking more of those dignified officers, the Swordbearer and Serjeant-at-arms, and although we smiled that day I for one – and I know the Dean too – was full of admiration for all the City's ancient titles and pageantry and the splendid work that lay behind it.

Later still I was indebted to the Dean for a tour of the White House in Washington. I was there on behalf of the Library Committee to support the Prince of Wales and the Dean in the opening of an exhibition of Christopher Wren's drawings for St Paul's Cathedral. On a free morning I joined the queue to see inside the White House and as the queue shuffled its way into the reception area, the Dean, very like Alice's white rabbit, popped out of a doorway, spotted me, and kindly took me in tow for a private tour led by the White House curator.

Two or three years after this when, with Ann, I was on a 'fire visit' to Washington, I had written to ask the curator whether we might visit and he kindly had us there on a Monday when the White House is closed to the public, so we had it all to ourselves and heard that his favourite first lady had been Jackie Kennedy.

Less agreeable was the City Lands Committee Dinner at Clothworkers Hall in November 1988 when half the diners – including ambassadors and other luminaries – went down next day with salmonella poisoning. Poor caterers, Ring & Brymer, had provided a flash-grilled savoury after the desert in which eggs were a constituent. The unfortunate among us had the bad eggs. The Lord Mayor escaped but the Lady Mayoress was afflicted as we learned the next day from our doctor who rushed from the Mansion House to my bedside to make me drink several pints of sugar water – the treatment not much better than the affliction. My malaise was slight, others much more serious. The Remembrancer suffered ill-effects for months and one of the diners never really recovered at all. This was the start of the upheaval in the egg-producing industry, Edwina Currie in charge of the programme to set new standards of hygiene.

An 800th Anniversary

This year saw the City celebrating the 800th anniversary of the mayoralty with a grand luncheon at Guildhall where the Queen, accompanied by Prince Phillip, proposed the toast to the Lord Mayor and the Corporation, saying that it was not just the length of time but the great record of achievement that was being celebrated.

As was the custom on such occasions a painting was commissioned and during the lunch, perched high upon a platform, the artist, Edward Hall was sketching the glittering scene laid out before him.

As the Chairman of the Libraries and Art Galleries Committee I had to satisfy myself that the painting, when finished, would be right. With Edwina Coven, who had been Chairman of the Reception Committee for the event, the Remembrancer and I went to Mr Hall's studio in Chelsea and were duly appalled. Right in the foreground, quite dominating the picture was a waiter carrying a tray. The Queen and the Lord Mayor and all the rest of us were dwarfed by this monstrous waiter. The artist was inclined to be touchy so the utmost tact was needed to persuade him that the waiter had to go. Alas poor Edward Hall, unwell, died before the painting was finished, and it was completed by Michael Reynolds, to grace the wall of the Old Library.

In 1989 came the creation by three Common Councilmen, Tom Wilmot, Michael Cassidy and Richard Saunders, of the City Architecture Forum, as a response to the Prince of Wales's plea for better buildings in the City. The idea was to bring together 'opinion formers' from among architects, developers, conservationists (I was one of these), financial institutions and the media, using seminars, presentations and conferences to promote better architectural performance – a useful initiative although I doubt whether His Royal Highness's hopes have been fulfilled!

The year ended on a high note with Hugh Bidwell, the new Lord Mayor, welcoming Prime Minister Margaret Thatcher at his banquet in November. In her speech she said that the only really bright spot in Britain's trade performance came from the City.

23

DETTA AT THE BARBICAN CENTRE, MORE LABOUR MACHINATIONS AND I AM MASTER OF OUR WARD CLUB

Detta O'Cathain took up her position as the new Director of the Barbican Centre early in 1990. I met her for the first time when she attended the opening of one of our exhibitions in the Art Gallery – I think it may have been the Lowry retrospective – and became one of her admirers. Ann and I saw her frequently, often sitting just behind her in the Corporation's complementary stalls seats in the Barbican concert hall.

Alas, as the years passed her style of management was not to everyone's liking. She had problems with the Royal Shakespeare Company (probably their fault rather than hers) and she departed within five years. During her time with us, Detta was appointed a life peer and, since she was a Corporation officer, sat on the cross benches. After she left the Barbican Centre she was able to take the Conservative whip and became Tory arts spokesman.

We had the first proposals for a complete refurbishment of the Mansion House which it badly needed. The cost would be £21 million and would entail one Lord Mayor having to miss being in the Mansion House for most of his year, moving into an attractive but far less grand house at 11 Ironmonger Lane. The Lord Mayors next in line were not over keen and the start of the project was delayed. Eventually it would be Lord Mayor Frank McWilliams who bit the bullet – more of that later.

Another, even more wide-ranging refurbishment, a £50 million scheme to modernise the meat market at Smithfield was mooted that year. This, too, was becoming urgent to meet hygiene requirements but again there were delays in starting. Was it really sensible to retain a wholesale market bang in the middle of a city?

The spring saw another three attempts by the Labour Party to get rid of the City Corporation. In March an unholy alliance of the left-wing Association of Local Authorities, Tower Hamlets, Hackney and the Greater London Labour Party, proposed that the Corporation be abolished and its functions (and cash) shared out among the neighbouring Labour-controlled councils. They kindly said that Guildhall would be retained as headquarters for some new London-wide body. The scheme was rejected by the Boundary Commission which said that the City's existence was guaranteed by statute.

The Corporation's rather more sensible suggestion was to ask that the Tower of London should become part of the City – but this proposal was also turned down by the Commission.

A rather more telling response to Labour's insistence on ending the City Corporation's existence came from the 700 Corporation tenants of the nearby

Golden Lane estate which was within Islington. They petitioned the Commission to change the boundary line so that they could escape Islington's clutches and become part of the Square Mile. 'We think ourselves part of the City' said their petition. This change was to be approved by the Boundary Commission and it provided me with the opportunity in Common Council to congratulate Golden Lane and welcome the 700 new City voters into my own Ward of Cripplegate.

In May, Tony Banks kept Labour's campaign going with a bill in the House of Commons to abolish the Corporation but allowing the Lord Mayor to stay in the Mansion House, the difference being that he would no longer be elected by the City's livery companies and Court of Aldermen but 'directly elected' by Londoners. Of course this bit of nonsense was dismissed as were all of Labour's other crackpot ideas.

But the Left were nothing if not persistent. In August, the City of London and Westminster South Labour Party put down their own motion for City abolition at the Labour Party Conference in Blackpool. Their ten-point plan was that the City Police should be merged with the Met; the City's housing estates would go to the boroughs in which they were situated as would the City-owned open spaces in and around London, with Hampstead Heath and Epping Forest to be taken over by the National Trust (!); the City's port health services given to the Department of the Environment or Ministry of Agriculture; traffic control responsibilities to the Department of Transport; the City's bridges to the Port of London Authority; the Honourable the Irish Society dissolved; and, finally, the Lord Mayor not to get a knighthood. This packet of absurdities was accepted by a show of hands at Blackpool but nothing ever came of it.

My own 1990, in addition to Corporation jobs – Chairman of the Libraries Committee, Governor of the Museum of London and Governor of the City of London School for Girls – had all manner of other excitements. One of the most interesting was to be Master that year of the Cripplegate Ward Club, the event inaugurated with a fine luncheon in the Old Library, Guildhall, attended by Lord Mayor Hugh Bidwell and his wife Jenny, and Sheriff Derek Edwards and his wife Julie.

In my speech proposing the toast to the Lord Mayor, Sheriffs and City Corporation, I expressed the hope that there would be a revival of interest in the Ward on the part of the numerous business houses which still abounded in Cripplegate.

> More than a century after the club was founded the voting pattern has swung right back to what it had been in the early and mid 1800s. Now, as then, it is almost exclusively the residents who provide the input into the City's government. Eleven of the twelve Common Councilmen for Cripplegate are Barbican residents whereas when I came to live here twenty years ago we had twelve businessmen to represent us.

We followed this initiative up with a reception at BP's Britannic House headquarters hosted by BP's Managing Director Ray Knowland. In my remarks to Ward members and specially invited people from firms in Cripplegate, I made the point that while the City continued as a separate entity of London government, having its unique business vote, it was wrong that so few business people in the Ward took any interest in civic affairs.

This meeting which discussed a wide range of City activities – rates, the amount of building work going on, how to get on the electoral roll and provision of another lending library – was something of a pioneering effort. Alas, it did not result in much new participation by our business firms in civic affairs but it was a starting point for all those 'consultation' projects which the City is offered these days – perhaps more than we really need!

The great event of our Ward Club year was the annual banquet held in 1990 at the old Haberdashers' Hall in Noble Street. My chief guest and speaker was Sir James Miskin, just retired as the Recorder of London, the senior judge at the Central Criminal Court and one who plays a major role in City ceremonial. That night he let his hair down and advocated an early return to flogging and hanging – policies which although welcomed by some of those present, did not go down too well with others. A great chap!

Having retired in 1989 as Director of the Fire Protection Association, I almost immediately took on a new job as Director-General of the new Arson Prevention Bureau, a joint enterprise by the insurance industry and the government to combat the steadily rising number of fires being started deliberately – an area of crime which had hitherto received little serious attention. I had already become the President of a European Arson Prevention Institute which ran seminars in Brussels and Luxembourg attended by fire, police, insurance and various other interests from all the European Union countries.

Briefly away from Guildhall to preside at a seminar in Luxembourg of the European Arson Prevention Institute

In May 1990 the Society of Fire Protection Engineers in the United States, with typical American generosity, awarded me their accolade of 'Fire Protection Man of the Year', an honour normally bestowed on Americans. Alas, I was unable to get to the awards banquet in San Antonio to bask in this glory.

I used to say that all these City and fire jobs were easily accommodated in the working week because I lived half way between my office in Aldersgate Street and the Guildhall and when necessary could get from one to the other by walking very quickly – or occasionally running!

24

NEW ARCHITECTURE AWARD; ATALI'S BANK MAKES US WONDER; AND A 'FINAL' LABOUR THREAT TO THE CITY

The Corporation's reputation for favouring building development (not always sympathetic to the City's character) is all too well-deserved but there is another side to the story that critics tend to overlook – the guardianship of so many listed buildings and the maintenance of its conservation areas.

At the start of 1991 it was recommended to Common Council that conservation areas be further enlarged and thus to cover 40% of our square mile. Not all the members approved – and outside in the property world there was probably a gnashing of teeth – but the Planning Chairman's proposal won the day easily enough.

The still new Chartered Architects livery, led by my friend the former City Architect, Stuart Murphy, and prompted no doubt by the Prince of Wales's justified dislike of recent buildings approved for the City, decided to inaugurate an annual award to encourage higher standards. Stuart invited the City Heritage Society to be joint sponsor, the new scheme to be closely modelled on our successful City Heritage Award for refurbishment projects.

The first of these 'New City Architecture' awards was presented in April 1991 by Lord Mayor Michael Graham for the pleasing 'Whitefriars' building just off Fleet Street, an early contribution to City architecture by Japanese developer Kumagai Gumi. Speaking at the ceremony I said: 'Those of us who work and live in the City have been depressed by the mediocrity, if not the downright ugliness of so many of our new buildings. This award is a positive step towards encouraging the high standards of design that befit the heart of a great capital city.'

Fine words, and I am sure the (almost) annual awards have been beneficial, but I sometimes wonder whether they have also encouraged developers to seek out the 'fashionable' architects of the day rather than employ the more workaday ones who design to suit the City's character rather than to demonstrate their own egos.

It was rather nice that our City Heritage Award was taken that summer by Seifert's – not an architectural practice noted for its interest in old buildings – for their commendable restoration of Rectory House, a merchant's residence of 1670, down by Lawrence Pountney churchyard. A rather good neoclassical scheme for new buildings to replace shabby-looking Paternoster by St Paul's was submitted by three architects – John Simpson, Terry Farrell and Richard Beeby – but alas it did not find favour with the City Planners although I believe it to have been even better than the quite good scheme we would eventually finish up with.

A letter was published in the *City Recorder* attacking the proposal that Finsbury Circus, the City's largest (and best) open space, should be used to deposit spoil from the underground workings of the proposed 'Crossrail' route linking the City, West End and Heathrow. The City's only small park would, as a result, be virtually destroyed and lost for three years. This threat remains although with the passage of the years and with the estimate of cost billioning ever higher I could not see it ever being built.

The Corporation's proposal for a £50 million refurbishment of the Smithfield meat market soon ran into trouble. Another letter in the *City Recorder* echoed the view of a good many people in suggesting that the market should be moved out of the City chiefly on the grounds that the big lorries coming in and out of these narrow streets were objectionable. 'Use the buildings to rehouse the Museum of London,' said the writer.

There were more serious problems at the end of 1991 when the market tenants overwhelmingly rejected the Corporation's scheme for refurbishment complaining that rents, rates and service charges would be excessive. I am glad to say that the Central Markets Committee and the Corporation as a whole kept its nerve. Eventually the refurbishment was successfully completed, the old system of meat carcasses hanging on open display replaced with temperature-controlled areas in steel and glass, the whole scheme beautifully contained within the splendid Victorian buildings – a worthy recipient of our City Heritage Award in 1995.

Opposite the market Barts Hospital also had its problems in 1991 making a second attempt to escape the clutches of the National Health Service by becoming a self-governing trust. Alas, the proposal was again turned down by the City and Hackney Community Health Council. A far worse fate was by then looming on the horizon.

Another notable event was the closing in July of the Mansion House for a two-year programme of total internal refurbishment, the Lord Mayor being re-housed at 11 Ironmonger Lane. Common Councilmen had the opportunity to purchase some of the furniture which it had been decided was surplus to requirements and Ann and I have as a souvenir a trolley that had been used to serve drinks on the upstairs balcony at summer parties.

The main recipient of goodies was our esteemed Guildhall Club manageress, Doreen, who, squirrel-like, managed to acquire some splendid pieces with which she transformed our club premises. They are there still and looking as good as ever.

London was not chosen as a home for many of the new agencies set up as adjuncts to the European Commission and, in 1991, there was some early satisfaction that the City would become the home of the new European Bank for Reconstruction and Redevelopment, its job being to help Eastern bloc countries with loans. The Director was the ebullient Frenchman Jacques Atali. A large (and costly) reception was provided in Guildhall to celebrate the Bank's inauguration. Over the next two or three years there was something of a reaction following Monsieur Atali's gold-plated decoration and furnishing of his lavish new premises in Broadgate and a constant demand for City hospitality for the Bank's frequent parties attended by a vast number of delegates from the eastern European countries. The following year Lord Mayor Sir Brian Jenkins made a bid for the City to get the rather more solid European Central Bank but that one fell to Germany.

My election address at the end of 1991 highlighted what I called the biggest threat to the City in many years:

> The Labour Party has declared that if it wins the General Election in 1992 [as everyone expected it would], it will, as part of its plan to reintroduce a Mark 2 Greater London Council, abolish the City of London Corporation. The likely outcome would be for the City's residents and businesses to be handed over to Islington. Eight hundred years of history would be scrapped. The City as the world's leading financial centre would be submerged. For Barbican residents the prospects would be unutterably grim. The Councilmen you elect would be no more.

Battle lines were drawn. In March 1992, 41,000 residents and businesses voiced their opposition to such a development. Labour stalwarts John Smith and Gwyneth Dunwoody who lived in the Barbican were asked to help. Even Arthur Scargill, another resident, was approached. The Labour Party was sufficiently impressed to drop the abolition threat from its manifesto. In any event Neil Kinnock's bid for glory failed and to the surprise of many John Major and the Conservatives were returned for another five years. Labour were not to be in office until 1997 by which time wiser councils had prevailed. We got the Mark 2 Greater London Council but the City Corporation was spared. And whilst the City continues to lay its golden eggs, providing the UK economy with such a vast amount of wealth, I am sure the threat will not return. One remains conscious, however, that it may not have gone away for all time!

In 1991, our Cripplegate Alderman, Sir Allan Davis, retired from the Court of Aldermen. Gavyn Arthur, a barrister who had already served as Councilman for the ward of Farringdon Without stood for the aldermanic vacancy in Cripplegate and was returned unopposed. Thus began another distinguished period with Gavyn becoming Sheriff in 1998 and Lord Mayor in 2002 – as well as a long-standing friend.

25

YEAR OF THE BOMBS; BARTS HOSPITAL; AND THE CITY CHURCHES UNDER THREAT

The year 1992 was to bring new threats to the City and its institutions.

In March the IRA planted a bomb outside the Crown Prosecution Service's building in Furnival Street. There was little damage and injuries to people were only slight – but it was a warning of worse to come.

On a Friday night in the middle of April another IRA bomb attack killed three people, injured ninety others, almost totally destroyed the great Baltic Exchange in St Mary Axe and badly damaged another twelve buildings including the magnificent Bevis Marks synagogue. Destruction was put at £1.5 billion.

Lord Mayor Sir Brian Jenkins and Chief Commoner Peter Rigby were seen on television the next day walking through the devastated streets, the Lord Mayor promising that the City would be ready for work again on Monday morning – as indeed it was.

There was to be another IRA attack in July when a bomb contained in a briefcase exploded beneath a Mercedes sports car outside the Chase Manhattan

Bank in Coleman Street. That signalled the end of the IRA activity until an even worse onslaught a year later.

We faced threats of another kind too, the most serious of them being to the future of St Bartholomew's, our 900-year-old hospital that had proved of such vital importance on so many occasions, most recently in treating the victims of the IRA bomb outrage.

For some time Whitehall ministers had been seeking ways to reduce the number of hospitals, particularly in London, and to encourage the creation of mega-units. The 'Tomlinson Report' in 1992 provided them with ammunition and Health Secretary Virginia Bottomley would be the one to grasp the nettle despite its obvious unpopularity. Barts, in her view, should be the main casualty: 'I am not in the business of conservation of elderly buildings,' were the unfortunate words she chose to justify her proposals. My own words were rather more to the point:

> My feeling is that Tomlinson has got it wrong and that we should, under no circumstances, allow this great hospital to die. We know that its outpatients' clinics are full each day, as are its inpatient beds. It is a splendid institution because of its medical and research facilities and its loss would be a tragedy, not just for City residents but for the hundreds of thousands who work in the City and for our neighbours in Islington and Hackney.

Tomlinson's proposals, to axe four London hospitals and thus to cut hospital beds by a quarter (down from around 20,000 to 15,000) and dispose of some 500 consultants, met with a wave of public indignation. A massive petition was handed in at 10 Downing Street, 3,000 people marched in protest from Barts to St Paul's and twenty-four-hour vigils were held in the hospital church of St Bartholomew the Less. Strangely enough, little, if anything, was being said by the City Corporation with its particular interest in one of the City's most important assets. Looking back now I believe this failure to bring its big guns into play right at the start must have encouraged Bottomley and her colleagues to feel that they could get away with it. In 1992 I feel certain that a sufficiently robust protest from the Corporation could have persuaded John Major to think again. My own attempt to bolster the Corporation's attitude did not come until 1994, but more of that later.

Also under threat in 1992 were the City's thirty-four churches. When in June Lord Templeman, who really should have known better, said in a report commissioned by the Church that there were far too many and that either new uses would have to be found for them (e.g. as halls for livery companies without one of their own) or they would need to be closed down. Shades of Alderman Sir Edward Howard's remark twenty years earlier that it would be a good idea to ship some of the churches, stone-by-stone, to the United States!

There was an immediate rallying-round to save all the churches under threat and their eventual reprieve would be announced by a new Bishop of London, Richard Chartres, a year or so later. The newly established 'Friends of the City Churches' did much to ensure that churches without a Sunday congregation would be open during weekdays for services, music, and as places where City workers and the many visitors to the City could find peace, quiet and beauty.

The proposed Guildhall Art Gallery building on the east side of Guildhall Yard was given its final go-ahead in 1992 although its £38 million budget, as was to be expected, would somewhat exceed that figure. Another Corporation success was that the long-running dispute with the Crown Estate as to the ownership of our Smithfield property, was settled to our satisfaction, the judgement being that three Royal Charters – Henry VI's in 1444, Henry VII's in 1505 and Charles I's in 1638 – were sufficient to prove the City's ownership.

Privatisation was still the economic order of the day and Guildhall staff – not just the manual workers but those in the legal, information technology and administrative grades – saw the government's introduction of 'compulsory competitive tendering' as something of a threat since it would require local authorities to put virtually all their work out to tender 'in order to ensure value for money'.

Another worry was the report of a rising water table with its special threat to tunnels and buildings in the City where levels were increasing faster than in other parts of London. The government would be asked to contribute to a £30 million programme for the sinking of boreholes all over London.

Our incoming Lord Mayor was Alderman Frank McWilliams and just before his assumption of office, Wyn, his wife, was knocked over by a motorcycle while she was shopping in Oxford Street. She suffered serious head injuries but by the greatest good fortune she made a remarkably speedy recovery and although not fit enough to take part in the Lord Mayor's Show, she was able to watch from the gallery in Guildhall part of the banquet on Monday 16 November. Happily she was very soon able to join the Lord Mayor in the as ever hectic programme of events – a programme in which Ann and I would also be playing a big part.

During the last months of 1992 the Guildhall 'kingmaker' Bunny Morgan, together with Edwina Coven who, on this occasion, would make common cause with Bunny, had decided that I would be the next Chief Commoner. It was an honour I had not expected but was more than willing to go for. The decision was in the hands of the City Lands and Bridge House Estates Committee, comprising the senior members of Common Council, who would elect their new Chairman early in January – usually there was more than one contender for the job which carried with it the title of Chief Commoner.

In December, an emissary visited me in my office on behalf of another candidate asking me to withdraw from candidature on the grounds that the other man had been in the running longer than me and would be preferred by the Lord Mayor since they were both members of the Loriners' livery company. My reply was that we should leave it to the City Lands Committee to make the choice, and there it would rest until the big day.

26

THE YEAR AS CHIEF COMMONER; VISIT TO WARSAW; ENTERTAINING LORD MAYORS FROM DUBLIN AND AUSTRALIAN CITIES; THE IRA BOMB AND ITS AFTERMATH

Wednesday 13 January 1993: to Guildhall for the first meeting of the year of the City Lands and Bridge House Estates Committee whose members, the most senior of the Common Councilmen, will shortly choose their new Chairman who, as leader of the City Council, enjoys the title of Chief Commoner.

This year there are three contenders – Derek Balls my fellow Cripplegate Deputy, Rodney Fitzgerald ('Fitz' to his many friends), and me. We three attend the 'call-over' ahead of the meeting proper so that we can listen-in (and participate) as the outgoing chairman goes through the agenda item by item with the officers.

The Committee assembles, almost immediately proceeding to the election. The Town Clerk reads out the names of all thirty-five members of the Committee, Aldermen and Common Councilmen, and each of the three contestants announces his willingness to serve as Chairman. Two commissionaires hand out voting slips and the votes are collected in two glass bowls and counted by the sitting Chairman who calls out the names on the slips. Not too many votes for Balls but Fitzgerald's and Woodward's names more or less alternate: Balls 4, Fitzgerald thirteen, Woodward fourteen. So there is a re-run. Peter Revell Smith whispers in my ear 'you only need half of Derek Balls's votes to be home and dry!' The result is, in fact, rather more favourable: Woodward 18, Fitzgerald 13.

With 'my' Lord Mayor Frank McWilliams; 1993 would be a hectic year for both of us

Applause as one takes the chair, Peter Rigby, my predecessor, tying the handsome Chief Commoner's badge of office around one's neck. The meeting goes with reasonable success – the Committee were forbearing. Then, with Peter Rigby, a quick look at the Chief Commoner's room and his flat in Guildhall West Wing. Later an 'audience' with Lord Mayor Frank McWilliams at the Mansion House and one knows it is going to be a happy relationship.

In the evening I fulfilled a long-promised engagement at London Fire Brigade headquarters and made a quick getaway to attend the very first of the Chief Commoner's engagements, a dinner in St James's of our Policy Committee, wearing the badge and beginning to feel the importance of office!

I am indebted to Christopher Mitchell, one of my successors, for this appraisal of that office.

> For over 400 years the management of the property and land belonging to the citizens of the City of London – known as the City's Estate – has rested with the City Lands Committee of the Corporation of London. The Chairman of this Committee enjoys the courtesy title of Chief Commoner.
>
> The origin of the City's Estate lies in the Royal Charters of Henry VI (1444) and Charles I (1638) conferring 'all houses, messuages and edifices and their site and foundation, and all watercourses, gutters and easements which now are erected, built or enjoyed in, upon or under void grounds, wastes, commons, streets, ways or public places and in the banks, shores and wastes of the Thames.' The revenue from buildings now standing on this land provides the major part of the Corporation's private income.
>
> In 1969 the City Lands Committee was merged with the Bridge House Estates Committee which was responsible for managing the property and lands possessed by the Corporation for the maintenance of the City's four bridges across the Thames.

The City lands and Bridge House Estates Committee is responsible for the management of the Corporation's private assets and controls the major part of the Corporation's non-rates revenue. It is regarded as the premier committee of the Corporation. It follows that the Chairman of this committee has great influence throughout the Corporation and takes precedence over all other commoners.

The courtesy title of Chief Commoner came into use in the last part of the nineteenth century when at a presentation dinner in 1880 the immediate past chairman of City Lands was referred to as 'The late Chief Commoner'.

The Chief Commoner, as Chairman of the City Lands and Bridge House Estates Committee, acts as a trustee for the citizens in ensuring that the estate is preserved for their benefit now and in the future.

The year was undoubtedly the most demanding in my life – and Ann agreed that it was also the most enjoyable. The days were filled with engagements – meetings, lunches with speeches, dinners with speeches, hosting receptions and of course dealing with the day-to-day business of the City Lands Committee and its various offshoots. One also attended at least one meeting of most of our other Corporation Committees. In between times I continued to run the Arson Prevention Bureau.

At the full meetings of the Court of Common Council it is the Chief Commoner who takes the lead in much of the business, for example in proposing the provision of hospitality to visiting heads of state. Before each meeting of the Court the Chief Commoner lunched with the Lord Mayor and Sheriffs at

Ironmonger Lane (since the Mansion House was closed for refurbishment) to ensure that any controversial items on the agenda would be properly addressed. At five minutes to one, quickly back to Guildhall so that the Chief Commoner is at his place to welcome the Lord Mayor on his ceremonial arrival at 'one of the clock'.

To Warsaw with the Lord Mayor

In looking back over that hectic twelve months some events stand out. One of the most memorable for Ann and me was to accompany the Lord Mayor and Lady Mayoress, Frank and Wyn McWilliams, in June on an official visit to Poland, memorable from the moment our cars swept us to the VIP lounge at Heathrow and then to the waiting plane, our stay in Warsaw with the British Ambassador, and our lengthy visit to Lech Walesa in the presidential palace.

At home it was the Chief Commoner's responsibility to entertain the Lord Mayor of Dublin in February and, in the summer, the Lord Mayors from Australia's six state capital cities. These events started with 'working breakfasts' at the Savoy Hotel (where our visitors were lodged) and culminated in a theatre (*Les Miserables* for Dublin, *Miss Saigon* for Australia) and a very late supper back at the Savoy. At lunch for the Australian mayors at the National Maritime Museum, instead of yet another speech I sang (not very well) a different version of 'Waltzing Matilda' with allegedly the original words from a British army recruiting song of the eighteenth century. Our guests took it well – probably having drunk almost as much as me.

At the Irish Embassy with the Lord Mayor and Lady
Mayoress of Dublin, the Ambassador and his lady

Chairing a breakfast meeting at the Savoy for the mayors
of the six Australian state capital cities

The Bomb

There had been a devastating interruption to City life on 24 April when the IRA drove a van into Bishopsgate and exploded a bomb outside the Hong Kong and Shanghai Bank, killing one man, injuring forty-four and causing £1 billion of damage. That was on a Saturday morning and on the Sunday, accompanied by Corporation officials, I walked through the glass from hundreds of shattered office windows along Bishopsgate. Perhaps the single most affecting sight was that of tiny St Ethelburga's, a church that had survived the Fire of London in 1666 and the Blitz, now almost totally destroyed. St Botolph's, St Helen's and All Hallows were damaged as was again the beautiful synagogue in Bevis Marks. The National Westminster tower, which had suffered £600,000 of damage in the previous year's bomb, was again shattered, in common with many other office buildings.

By the Monday the City was back at work, alternative premises having been found for the thousands of staff whose offices had been wrecked, although Bishopsgate itself would remain closed to traffic for weeks.

There was one far-reaching effect. Some of the businessmen whose premises had been badly damaged, led by Lord Alexander, Chairman of the National Westminster Bank, were demanding a far greater degree of protection from terrorist attack which, unless the City could provide it, might force them to relocate away from the City. The challenge was taken up by Michael Cassidy, Chairman of our Policy and

Aftermath of the IRA bomb in Bishopsgate
Picture courtesy of Guildhall Library

Resources Committee who, with Owen Kelly, the City Police Commissioner, set about preparing plans for road closures and police checkpoints to limit entry into the central area of the City, plans resulting in what the newspapers would call the 'Ring of Steel'.

It did seem to me that our proposed measures were possibly over-draconian and I voiced my concern at a meeting at Guildhall attended by Lord Alexander and other leading City figures. The Commissioner of Police had already said that roadblocks and closure of streets were matters for government decision but Michael Cassidy's plans moved ahead rapidly.

Not everyone was overjoyed, least of all Home Secretary Kenneth Clarke and Prime Minister John Major, who felt that the City was taking too much upon itself. At a reception around that time in the Guildhall Crypts a message came through to the Lord Mayor from Detta O'Cathain telephoning from the House of Lords. I was asked to speak to her and she told me that the Prime Minister, complaining bitterly about the 'Ring of Steel', had asked: 'who will rid me of this turbulent priest?' or words to that effect. Eventually our road closures were grudgingly accepted, helped by the excuse that they were not security matters at all but part of a long-awaited scheme for 'environmental improvements'. The plus-factor is that the 'Ring of Steel' with its network of CCTV cameras at each of the entries to the City has discouraged not only terrorists but more humdrum criminals from entering our streets with a noticeable drop in the crime rate.

Let Festivities Recommence

Long before the Bishopsgate rubble was cleared the City was well and truly back in full swing with a glittering banquet for the President of Portugal and as the 'mover of the resolution' that the Corporation should provide this hospitality I found myself in possession of the medal and star of that country's Order of Merit – with permission later received from the Queen to wear them on suitable occasions.

We also gave banquets in 1993 to the presidents of Colombia and the Ukraine and held receptions in Guildhall for the Royal Air Force, the Royal Naval Volunteer Reserve, the English Speaking Union and the London Court of International Arbitration. All enormously enjoyable for Ann and me – but the Chief Commoner's life is not just a succession of parties; there are many serious moments too, and even a Guildhall banquet can have difficult consequences, as is revealed in the following chapter.

Ann and I welcome the head of the Army Benevolent Fund and his lady to an evening reception in Guildhall

27

HOSPITALITY HICCUP; PREVIEW OF THE CHANNEL TUNNEL; GIVING THE LORD MAYOR THE KEY OF THE DOOR

The banquet for the President of Colombia, Cesar Augusto Gaveria, was on Tuesday 27 July. At its conclusion, when we were waving him off from the Guildhall porch, it was clear that the Lord Mayor was not best pleased.

At nine the next morning his private secretary, Air Vice-Marshal Michael Dickin, phoned to ask me, urgently, to come over to Ironmonger Lane. On my arrival he told me that the Lord Mayor was threatening to resign over what he considered to have been an affront at the Banquet. I was ushered into the presence of a still highly irate Frank McWilliams.

What had gone wrong was that when the Colombian President had risen to deliver his speech (in Spanish) the Lord Mayor – probably the only person among the 700 or more people in Guildhall – did not have an English translation in front of him, and it was quite a long speech! He held the Remembrancer and the Chairman of the Reception Committee to blame. They had to apologise.

While I am sure the Lord Mayor had not the slightest intention of resigning it seemed to me that whatever the rights and wrongs of the matter, apologies were vital. I invited Adrian Barnes, the Remembrancer, and Richard Saunders, Chairman of the Reception Committee to my room in Guildhall and explained the situation to them. Both felt themselves to be totally blameless of any involvement in the missing translation but eventually for the sake of peace, both agreed to write letters of apology. Later that day both were seen by the Lord Mayor and all was again sweetness and light in Ironmonger Lane and Guildhall.

The previous month had been full of activity. On 7 June I joined the Lord Mayor and Lady Mayoress in LM0, the mayoral Rolls Royce, for a preview of the nearly completed Channel Tunnel through which we travelled for a mile or two in a sort of trolley on rails. All very impressive but it did occur to me while we had our sandwiches and orange juice later on that we would have done better gastronomically at the Calais end.

Especially enjoyable was the unveiling two days later of the Silver Jubilee panoramic panels on London Bridge. On a lovely summer's day, the west-facing plaque in the middle of the bridge was unveiled by the Duke Gloucester. That facing east was unveiled by the Chief Commoner, the traffic halted to allow him to cross to the other side. Fame at last with one's name inscribed there for posterity! Lord Mayor, Duke and I were whisked back for a celebratory lunch in the Guildhall Crypt.

Four months later, when a splendid new exhibition opened on Tower Bridge in commemoration of its centenary there was another plaque naming the Chief Commoner in the entrance to the exhibition. Alas, hopes of further immortality on Southwark and Blackfriars Bridges were never realised!

Unveiling a panoramic panel on London Bridge

But in July, thanks to an initiative by my successor as Director of the Fire Protection Association, it was the Chief Commoner who unveiled a plaque naming an alleyway off Aldersgate Street as 'Braidwood Passage' commemorating that famous fireman who led the London Fire Engine Establishment from 1832 until his death in 1861 fighting a devastating fire in Tooley Street, Southwark.

One of the happiest events at this time was the reopening on the first of September of the Mansion House after its extensive refurbishment. We marked the occasion in great style, the Chief Commoner (as owner-custodian) handing over the large key to the front door to the Lord Mayor and then all of us trooping in for a tour of inspection. Inside was magnificence on a lavish scale, a tribute to Bill Row, the Corporation's Director of Building and Services, architect Donald Insall, and a host of master craftsmen.

A few days later we tried out how the practical arrangements of the house would actually work with a trial dinner in the Egyptian Hall with our Aldermen and Common Councilmen as the critical diners, and the Lord Mayor and me trying out the new sound system as the speakers. All seemed to think that the house was quite ready for the first of the many banquets to come.

Giving Barbican Residents a Voice

Over many years a constant complaint among Common Councilmen representing the Barbican wards of Aldersgate and Cripplegate had been the Corporation's ruling that they could not serve on the Barbican Residential Committee nor, indeed, speak in Common Council on Barbican matters because of possible conflict of interest. This ruling was enshrined in Corporation Standing Order 66.

As Chief Commoner one had a golden opportunity to draw the attention of Common Council to what we considered the absurdity of this ruling and twice during 1993, with apologies to the Lord Mayor, I rose in my place in Common Council and walked out of the Chamber when items affecting the Barbican came up on the agenda. On each occasion I was followed by every Cripplegate and Aldersgate member – all nineteen of us plus Councilmen for other wards who lived in the Barbican.

The particular occasion was a debate on whether or not residents should contribute to a proposed £1.8 million refurbishment of the Barbican ventilation system – mainly to protect against spread of fire. Since with my own knowledge of fire safety I was convinced that the measures proposed were entirely unjustified and a waste of money (but was prevented by Standing Order 66 from explaining this to Common Council) it seemed that a well-behaved 'demo' was the answer.

The demonstration worked and Sam Jones, the Town Clerk, was able shortly afterwards to persuade the Policy Committee of the need for sensible revision of the offending standing order. Arrangements were made for we Cripplegate and Aldersgate members to sit on the Barbican Residential Committee and thus to make available our own personal knowledge of Barbican management issues. I was also pleased that we were able to persuade the Committee to scrap the costly plans in respect of fire safety.

Without Honour

I must mention another bit of business with some far-reaching and unfortunate effects. Michael Cassidy, our Policy Chairman, and I were invited one day to visit the Lord Mayor who told us that the Prime Minister, John Major, had phoned him to say that as part of his plans to make the honours system 'more democratic' (recognising the worth of school caretakers and lollipop ladies, etc.) he was proposing that from now on Lord Mayors would no longer be appointed GBE (Knight Grand Cross of the Most Excellent Order of the British Empire) upon their taking up office in November. Any honour would come later, depending on their performance. Did we two have any observations on this? We gathered that the Prime Minister required an urgent response. Faced with this somewhat revolutionary idea (Lord Mayors had been getting their automatic knighthoods for a long time) we – rather inadequately I think in retrospect – had little to offer. Looking back we should at least have asked the Lord Mayor whether he was also consulting his fellow Aldermen.

The outcome was that Frank McWilliams would be the last Lord Mayor to have a GBE and the last to be honoured at the beginning of his year. Henceforth the honour would be a simple knighthood bestowed at the end of the mayoralty.

There was much indignation in the City about what came to be seen as a slight on the historic office of the mayoralty. After all, in becoming Lord Mayor, an Alderman had already spent twelve years in devoted service to the City and had surely by then earned his recognition. Additionally in his worldwide ambassadorial duties, it was clearly an advantage for a Lord Mayor to have the added clout of a knighthood.

But all this is water under the bridge, with Mr Major's 'reforms' enthusiastically developed by Mr Blair. One cannot see any changes for the better in the foreseeable future.

The Chief Commoner's year was in its final quarter but there remained some treats.

More Banquets

In October, we had our grand City Lands Dinner at Mercers Hall with a host of distinguished guests – the Lord Mayor and Lady Mayoress of course, the Sheriffs, Masters of Livery Companies to whom I could repay their abundant hospitality to me, friends from the worlds of property and architecture, Ambassadors from countries with which we had special dealings during the year, and a contingent from Buckingham Palace and the Foreign Office led by Sir James Weatherall, the Marshal of the Diplomatic Corps.

I had arranged with Earl Ferrers, Minister of State at the Home Office, that he would be our chief guest that night and reply to the toast to the guests. At the eleventh hour he telephoned to say that ministers in the Lords had all been 'whipped' to take part in a debate where the voting balance was in doubt.

We phoned Sir James Weatherall to ask if at very short notice he would consent to sing for his supper. He said he had never done anything quite of this kind but was willing to have a go. He 'sang' beautifully and told me at a later date that the City Lands event had launched him on his public speaking career!

The last of the year's treats was to ride in a coach, a marvellous way of travelling, as part of the new Lord Mayor's Show on Saturday 13 November. Paul Newall was unfortunate in the weather, it being the wettest show for years, and I was grateful to be in a closed carriage so only got wet on our occasional stops such as the one at the Law Courts. In spite of the weather the City streets were lined with cheering people. Ann was waiting for me at the Mansion House having watched the procession from the balcony, the chill damp being kept at bay with a whisky or two. Then we had lunch in the Egyptian Hall.

On the Monday we had the banquet at Guildhall, the Lord Mayor, the Archbishop of Canterbury and the Lord Chancellor in full robes, all in good voice, with Prime Minister John Major telling us of his plans for the months ahead.

Later Ann and I joined the Lord Mayor, Lady Mayoress Penny, the Majors and a few others to be taken by coach to the Mansion House for final drinks. John Major, as always such an agreeable man (if not the most successful of Conservative leaders) was in a relaxed mood now. Norma Major told us that it really had been an ordeal for her having once again to process the length of the Old Library as she and the Prime Minister, the chief guest, were received by the Lord Mayor.

I had a break from the City the following week to give a talk in Barcelona to Spanish fire and security people about the increasing threat from arson.

Then a final few weeks of packed City engagements: Spitalfields Committee lunch at Haberdashers' Hall; meeting at Mansion House with our Brussels Ambassador; the Billingsgate Committee Dinner; Banquet of the City Livery Club in Guildhall; an exhibition in the Guildhall Library print room; St Paul's luncheon with the Dean in the Chapter House; the Glass Sellers livery dinner; the Lady Mayoress 'at home'; the Guild of Freemen Dinner at Guildhall; another speech at the Corporation Staff Christmas lunch party; visiting the Corporation's almshouses in Southwark and Brixton; dinner with the Establishment Committee; yet another dinner with the Housing Committee; and, finally, the candlelit carol service at St Lawrence Jewry with the Lord Mayor and so many others from the Court of Common Council partaking in this closing event of the year.

I would be handing over my responsibilities and badge of office to my successor, the greatly esteemed Councilman John Holland, on Wednesday 12 January. But just before that, on the Monday night, Ann and I gave a private dinner party in the Chief Commoner's Parlour at Guildhall for special friends of the year. Around the great table with its eighteen places we had Sam Jones the Town Clerk, Adrian Barnes the Remembrancer, Sheriffs Roger Cork and Tony Moss, John Lucioni the Keeper of the Guildhall, Major-General Tyler Governor of the Tower of London (where we had spent so much time), Roger Taylor representing the insurance world and its arson connections, and Rodger Whitelocke, a Barts consultant, to signify our special concern for that great City hospital. All had their wives with them, not only bringing glamour to the occasion but in recognition of their own contribution to the success and happiness of the year – as exemplified in the role played by my own wife, Ann.

28

WE SUFFER MR MUGABE AND TRY TO SAVE BARTS

In the first few days of 1994, I was still Chief Commoner, and proposing the toast to the Lord Mayor at the annual dinner for heads of the governing bodies of London – the mayors and leaders of the thirty-two boroughs (thank goodness no GLC following its abolition). It was always a privilege of the Chief Commoner to speak on these occasions until one ill-advised Lord Mayor, persuaded by Policy Chairman Judith Mayhew, killed off the custom for a year or two.

In fact the early weeks of this year were still extraordinarily full – lunch at the Old Bailey with the Judges; dinner at the Mansion House with the Bishops and then with the 'British Invisibles' financial leaders; Guildhall reception for the Lifeboat Institution, a few days break from the City to run a European arson seminar in Brussels; back for the Chartered Architects livery banquet at the Mansion House and enjoying an *en famille* luncheon with the Lord Mayor and Lady Mayoress plus an unexpected lunch with Lord Palumbo in his Walbrook fastness.

There was one entertainment that year we could

well have done without. The Foreign Office had, some months earlier, decided to inflict the President of Zimbabwe on the Queen (and the Corporation) for a state visit and, writing about it long after the event, even although the worst excesses of the Mugabe regime were still to come, the visit was not one of the Foreign Office's happiest of ideas – coming in the same category as our welcome for the Zaire contingent (see page 71) and that for Ceausescu of Romania.

In 1993 I had proposed the motion in Common Council for the Mugabe banquet and so on Wednesday 18 May was the first of those called on to mount the dais in the Old Library to be received by him. The custom of course was for the VIP to stand and shake your hand but Mugabe stayed rigidly in his chair. Fortunately for the others who followed me the Lord Mayor had nudged him into more polite behaviour.

The Attempt to Save Barts

However, for me, 1994 was the year for Barts. The threat to the hospital had become acute in July when the Royal Hospitals Trust set out plans to close Barts completely before the end of the century. Virginia Bottomley, the Secretary of State, fortified in her resolve by the Tomlinson Report (see page 173) and not discouraged by John Major, was all too willing to act.

Our last hope, it seemed to me, was to galvanise the City Corporation into action. So it was that in Common Council on 8 September 1994 I moved a resolution 'affirming our unwavering conviction of the need for hospital facilities at Smithfield' and calling for positive action by the Corporation to this end.

In a highly charged emotional atmosphere with the public gallery packed as never before or since, every chair occupied and the aisles packed – Barts consultants, doctors and nurses there in force – the resolution was passed with unanimous acclaim by the 120 Councilmen and Aldermen present in Guildhall that day. Here are some of the things I said in my speech:

> The Lord Mayor at his Guildhall Banquet received thunderous applause when he criticised hospital closures in London. When I referred to Barts in my farewell speech as Chief Commoner – that was the bit that won the greatest ovation. Virtually everyone wants Barts to continue. There were more than a million signatures in the petition delivered to Downing Street.
>
> The Corporation has failed to follow through on these expressions of concern. This Corporation, so powerful, so ready to support good causes, has been unaccountably silent on an issue of the utmost importance to the City and London as a whole. When we should have been roaring like a lion we have uttered no more than a squeak. This coyness has astonished our friends and contributed to the demoralisation of the staff at Barts. We should from the start, following the flawed recommendations of the Tomlinson Report, have made the government aware of our unwavering opposition to the closure of Barts.
>
> The City's case is strong. First, the enormous contribution the City makes to the national economy

is deserving of the hospital facilities expected in a world financial centre. Second, the case for reducing hospital beds in London is now totally discredited. Third, it is demonstrably crazy to put on the scrapheap the magnificent facilities at Barts recently updated at a cost of £60 million, some of the finest in Europe. Fourth, Barts is doing well not only in medical but in financial terms – the latest accounts showing a surplus of nearly £500,000. Barts is poised to provide services on a Europe-wide basis and to win substantial resources from the private sector.

Barts is older than Parliament, one of the oldest hospitals in the world and arguably the most famous. Lord Rees Mogg has said that if every hospital in the country had to be shut except one, Barts should be that one. We need to remind the government that it should show respect for national institutions of such outstanding excellence.

I argued that we should immediately set up a working party of people dedicated to the continuation of hospital facilities at Barts and to develop measures to that end. The working party would be led by Joyce Nash, Chairman of the Corporation's Health Committee (whose agreement I had obtained with a flow of telephone calls to her while she was holidaying in Madeira). Joyce, in seconding the resolution, said 'there was a perception that Barts was not a priority issue for the Corporation which was reluctant to condemn the actions of a Cabinet Minister – Virginia Bottomley – even when she was issuing edicts detrimental to the care of electors.'

The Secretary of State was immediately informed of

the Court of Common Council's decisions. The working party came quickly into being, comprising leading members of the Court, the heads of major City financial institutions and people with influential positions in the health service. Sir Evelyn de Rothschild was an early member. Joyce Nash was Chairman and I its Deputy Chairman. All seemed to be set fair.

Meanwhile Joyce and I invited our esteemed MP, Peter Brooke, to come and talk to us at Guildhall. During the course of that meeting I said to Peter that it seemed to me quite inconceivable that a Conservative government could preside over the destruction of a 900-year-old institution. He agreed and that it seemed reprehensible to him. Later, at the conclusion of the final debate on closure of Barts Peter Brooke would, for the only time in his long Parliamentary career, vote with Labour against his own party on this issue.

I might add that for Ann (a leading light in the Cities of London and Westminster South Conservative Party) and I, the killing of Barts caused us to withdraw from membership of the Party.

Back to Our Working Party

We needed expert help and had been advised (by our Town Clerk) that the Newchurch organisation, which specialised in work for hospitals, would provide a good consultancy. We gave them the task but discovered that their head, absurdly from our point of view, had no great personal love of Barts. Indeed one of the senior consultants at the hospital told me privately that we could not have made a worse choice!

Newchurch convinced us that, because of the entrenched position of the NHS which, after all, controlled the purse-strings, we could not hope for Barts to resume as a general hospital but that they could make a strong case for retention of clinical services there to serve residents in the City and round about and the City's working population.

Such a case was indeed made, the package of services including a new 'local' hospital, health care for the elderly, community mental health services, primary health care (via GP services), occupational health services for City workers and the City's own social services organisation.

The capital cost was estimated at between £5 and £6 million with total revenues of a like amount. There would be 180 full-time staff. The West Wing building at Barts would house the new facilities which later could include nursing home beds, rehabilitation services, alternative therapies and dental services.

It all looked reasonably promising. But it would depend on support forthcoming from the Royal Hospitals Trust, City and Hackney Community Services NHS Trust, Camden and Islington NHS Trust and from our own and neighbouring GP practices. Although the City Corporation itself remained fairly enthusiastic, the willingness of the other bodies to contribute financially was clearly waning, and what had started as a reasonably satisfactory solution to the City's health needs gradually faded away. The real problem of course was that the various NHS groups did not really want any kind of City hospital on the Barts site and although I still had hopes of sufficient City Corporation financial input, the kind of money required was beyond the City's means.

There were further attempts made to save Barts. A study commissioned by the King's Fund, London's health think tank argued that Barts should become a charitable foundation offering specialist services, still part of the NHS, although housing a private hospital as well.

Even better from our point of view was another set of proposals backed by Barts consultants for a charitable foundation but one with a much wider remit that would virtually recreate the old Barts, complete with A&E services.

But again these proposals foundered for lack of financial backing.

At least the government's plans to sell off the listed Barts buildings to the London School of Economics or a Japanese hotel happily came to nothing. In the fullness of time, with a new government in office there came hope for retaining hospital facilities there (one of the few good things stemming from New Labour). Eventually the whole of the West Wing was splendidly restored as a specialist cancer hospital with substantial financial input from the City, the rest of the site to be given over for cardiac and other care.

So at the end the NHS had to agree that Barts as well as the Royal London Hospital should be rebuilt and restored, the PFI (Private Finance Initiative) cost astronomically high. When these plans for the new Barts were put out for comment I made a plea that even at this late stage it would be right for the City's residents and workers that general medical care on a somewhat higher level than the existing minor injuries unit should be included as a small part of this vast undertaking. But how much more sensible it would have been to keep Barts as it was originally and add to it as later thought desirable!

29

AND IN CONCLUSION...

After holding high office in the City – be it Lord Mayor or even Chief Commoner – one should not be in too much of a hurry to leave the scene. Those who follow in your footsteps appreciate your being around for a while if only to tap into your experience. I stayed a member of the Court of Common Council for three years after my own spell of glory and might well have stayed longer still had my Ward of Cripplegate not become somewhat trying. But by the end of 1996 I had been on Common Council for twenty-five years and it seemed to me that enough was enough. Some of my friends at Guildhall were kind enough to say that my continued presence was important, but for me the die was cast, and at least one left on the crest of the wave. I was pleased that our neighbour and friend in the Barbican, Lionel Altman, was ready and willing to stand for Common Council, and Cripplegate was fortunate in having as its two Deputies John Barker and Stella Currie, both already having chaired committees and John on his way as I write to becoming another Cripplegate Chief Commoner.

Meanwhile there remained plenty of activity at Guildhall – and further afield. Particularly enjoyable was carrying out one of the City's regular inspections of old London Bridge, now situated at Lake Havasu City, Arizona.

To Lake Havasu

Readers may recall that Common Councilman Ivan Luckin had contrived to sell Rennie's bridge of 1831 to an American who had rebuilt it stone by stone in the Arizona desert, diverting a river which the bridge could span, and creating around it a new residential city and tourist attraction complete with English pub and souvenir shop.

I was accompanied by Town Clerk Sam Jones and his wife Jean (since we were travelling 'steerage' by air to Los Angeles I advised Ann to give this trip a miss).

*London Bridge at Lake Havasu, Arizona and, below,
Town Clerk Sam Jones and I take to the water*

We were given the warmest of welcomes at Lake Havasu. London Bridge in that crystal-clear Arizona air looked much more clean and sparkling than it had ever done across the Thames. Dinners and lunches galore and a nail-bitingly fast cruise on the lake and its river. The high spot was to ride in Lake Havasu's London Bridge Parade, perched precariously on the roof of a Ford Mustang, wearing my mazarine blue gown (temperature close on ninety degrees Fahrenheit) and a rather snazzy baseball cap, drum majorettes providing a guard of honour.

Ready for the Lake Havasu Parade, on board one of the forty Ford Mustangs taking part

In fact this inspection of the bridge turned out to be the very last in a series which had begun in the 1970s. At dinner one night the Mayor made it clear to me in the nicest possible way that the Lake Havasu dignitaries felt that they had provided sufficient hospitality for the City of London and what about a bit of reciprocity? I took it upon myself to assure him that an invitation for him and his entourage to visit us in London would soon be on its way. When we got home Sam Jones set the necessary wheels in motion.

In May 1996, the Lake Havasu party were put up at the Savoy, given a splendid luncheon at Cutlers Hall, were entertained by Petula Clark in *Sunset Boulevard* at the Adelphi, and had a farewell supper back at the Savoy.

The Blair Lecture

In September, the Corporation had the notion of inviting Tony Blair as leader of the Labour Party to present a lecture in Guildhall and he was given a fairly rapturous welcome by the large audience present. The Corporation, as has often been its wont, could see the way the political wind was blowing – indeed it did not take too much perception to see that the days of John Major's ministry were numbered.

We governors of the Museum of London had the task of appointing a successor as director to Max Hebditch, who had run the Museum so brilliantly since its opening. Our choice was Simon Thurley, who seemed to encompass in his career to date and his numerous extra-curricular activities an extraordinary wide range of talents. I asked him if he felt confident that he could keep so many balls in the air. We certainly made the right choice and his (all-too-brief) spell as director was very successful but the chance of becoming head of English Heritage could not be missed.

The City's architectural heritage was still a major preoccupation for me and I was arguing in Guildhall against the threat of controls being relaxed in our conservation areas allowing for replacement of good buildings with unsuitably large office blocks.

In my very last election address I warned that with the likelihood of a change of government there would once again be the very real threat of the City Corporation's abolition. In the outcome Mr Blair and his colleagues concluded that the Corporation was worth keeping, a decision that was certainly helped on its way by the efforts of Policy Committee's Michael Cassidy who had established a good relationship with Labour.

The Corporation's Heads of Policy

There have been for many years mixed feelings about our Policy Chairmen, not least because of the length of time they continue in office, six years as opposed to the normal three for other chairmen (and only one year for the Chief Commoner). In that lengthy period they tend to assume considerable power. Criticism was voiced during Peter Rigby's tenure of office and became more pronounced during Michael Cassidy's time, but reached its loudest almost from the start of Judith Mayhew's becoming Chairman, the main cause of complaint being that she often gave the impression that it was she, rather than the Lord Mayor, who was running the Guildhall show.

Judith was something of a phenomenon. Almost immediately after becoming a Councilman – she was elected in place of her husband – whenever she put her name forward for a committee appointment Judith got more votes than established members of the Court. Life was not always plain sailing though, and when I was Chief Commoner, Judith, in tears, complained that as Deputy Chairman of Policy, Chairman Michael Cassidy kept her in the dark about what was going on.

The most hilarious of events surrounding Judith was that she appeared in a video produced by New Zealand television for showing in that country, in which she was clearly depicted as Queen of the Common Council. Anyway, she more than maintained Michael Cassidy's love affair with New Labour and, indeed, established her own special relationship with Mayor Livingstone. On her final departure from the Court, armed with her DBE (nothing like this ever before given to previous Policy Chairmen) she successfully stormed the gates of academe (King's College Cambridge) and the Royal Opera House. Clearly a lady of some accomplishment.

Past Lord Mayors (and past Chief Commoners) continue to enjoy life, be it as Chairmen of the exclusive Guildhall Historical Association or as Mr Pickwick at the City Pickwick Club at the George and Vulture. At the latter I have long enjoyed the soubriquet of Jingle even to the extent when speaking there of attempting his strange style of delivery.

Still in Good Shape

Looking back over my years on Common Council and beyond I cannot but feel that despite some of the questionable changes and developments of recent years, the Corporation remains a good local authority, better in so many respects than its neighbour boroughs. Some would even argue that it is stronger and more powerful in terms of the admiration in which it is held by central government and on the international stage. If that is so it is due to the success of the City in amassing great wealth – wealth which goes to help keep the UK economy afloat. The danger is that if ever the golden eggs cease to be forthcoming, politicians at Westminster might once again think of killing the goose – a threat which, as I have recorded, has been such a constant theme over the years.